A STORY TO TELL

Charleston, SC
www.PalmettoPublishing.com

A Story to Tell

First Edition

Hardcover: 978-1-63837-562-3
Paperback: 978-1-63837-563-0
eBook: 978-1-63837-564-7

A STORY TO TELL

BY T. A. CASTA

CONTENTS

CHAPTER ONE

YOU KNOW HOW IN THE MOVIES WHEN SOMETHING TRAGIC HAPPENS, it seems to be night, rain pours down, and lightning flashes? I think I remember my former English teacher Mrs. Levine referring to this as "dramatic effect." But I am not in English class now. It is August, and I have just graduated from high school. I had been expected to head off to college in the fall like my best friend, Alyssa. But that will not happen either—in part because of her, or maybe that is not fair. I am not sure what is fair right now.

Another thing: it is not storming out. The sun is shining brightly on this late August afternoon. This is a tragic day, though. In this moment I feel like it is one of the worst days of my life, except maybe the day that led to me coming on this journey and the day that led to that too.

As I am riding in the car, one of my favorite movies flashes through my mind. Ironically, it is called *Riding in Cars with Boys,* starring Drew Barrymore and the late and great Brittany Murphy. Drew's character, Beverly, states, "All life is, is four or five big days that change everything." Have I had my four or five big days already?

I ponder this idea and what that would mean for me as I ride along in the car, the sun shines brightly and blinding me through the window. I close my eyes. I try to think of only the movie and not the drama that is my current life.

I am not riding in a car with boys, however. I am sitting in the front passenger seat opposite Kristen Ann Rogers, my mother. I open my eyes and glance quickly at my mother before she can notice. Her knuckles are white as she grips the steering wheel, concentrating on the road through puffy eyes.

My mother has been crying ever since the decision was made. I, however, have not given into the hot sting of tears that will surely come, most likely soaking into my pillow, and lost in the dark of the night. But as the sun shines bright, I will put on a brave face. It is not that I am happy with this decision, a decision that has been made for me, as opposed to by me. This is a decision that impacts my life. I am the one going away.

Maybe I want to go away, though. I certainly do want to escape. I have every day since graduation. That was the last day I remember feeling normal. Everything changed after that day. But I do not want to get into that now.

It has only been about an hour and a half since we set out on this journey. This means we have a little over two hours to go. I know this only from eavesdropping on my mother and Aunt Jenny as those plans had been set in motion for me and looking it up on Google search after. My Aunt Jenny is my mother's younger sister and the only relative she has left. My grandparents have passed, and there is not much family to speak of. As for my father's family, well, I would not even know them if they were sitting on a park bench right next to me. The fact is I would not even know my father if *he* were sitting on a park bench right next to me. I never met him. I do not even know if he knows about me, honestly. My mother does not talk about him, and I would not put it past her to not even tell him. She needs to be in control of everything. Of course, I know this is not completely true or fair. She is a bit controlling, but she is also kind and really a lot less strict than some of my friends' parents. I have also not been the same person over the last couple of months, and she does not know why. I am not her little Katrina Margaret Rogers anymore. Little Katrina had bony skinned up knees and big brown eyes full of wonder. The world is not a wondrous place anymore though because I have seen pain, I have felt pain, and I am living in pain right now at this moment. It is both the pain of what I have been through, and the pain of not being able to find the words to tell my mother. In doing so I am causing her pain, and I know this. However, what I do not know is how to stop the pain for either of us.

CHAPTER TWO

My choices over these past couple of months really must have pissed my mom off, most likely starting with the tattoo I got the day of graduation. It was of a blue butterfly on my chest. My intention was not to make myself "look cheap," as my mother had so kindly stated. I only intended to get the tattoo in a spot where I could cover it up for prospective jobs in the future. The butterfly was supposed to represent freedom. It is now ironic that I am going to a place where I will not be free at all.

I want to ask questions, like how long I will stay and how often my mother will visit. However, I am both afraid of the answer and unsure if my mother can even answer them. So, I sit in silence. We have two more hours to go. This is going to be a long ride.

All I have got to keep me company, aside from a silent and pissed-off mother, are my thoughts. This means I need to actively force myself to *not* think of the events that led up to this moment. I will go there later. I know this place I am going to will make me look at everything that has happened. It will most likely make me look at everything since my birth on June 15th, 2001 and evaluate it. How is it possible that I was celebrating turning seventeen only a couple of months ago? It feels like I have lived a lifetime since then. For now,

I try not to think of everything that has changed. Everything I have known has changed. I have changed.

Even my appearance has changed. I still stand at five foot three. Aside from height, everything else has gotten smaller. Even my hair has gotten smaller. My wavy brown hair that once reached down to my lower back, now barely touches my shoulders.

I cut my hair after graduation night. I had cut it for so many reasons. As I stepped into the shower after and ran my fingers so easily through my hair, it had felt like taking some control back. Looking back, I see how foolish this was. It is, after all, just hair. I do not miss it, though. Among the things I miss, my hair is not one of them.

I close my dark brown eyes once again, trying to shut out the thoughts that are threatening to show themselves. "So, you are just going to sleep while I drive?" my mother asks, interrupting my thoughts.

I have not decided if I am happy for the interruption or not. I respond anyway. "No, Mother, the sun just got into my eyes. I am awake."

"This is not a punishment, you know. You need to do this."

I am not sure who she says this for, her or myself.

I do know I need to respond again, though. "I know" is all I say. It seems to be enough. Once again, only my thoughts keep me company. Over the next two hours, neither of us speaks again. By the time we pull up to the gate I am exhausted from my thoughts. Once past the gate, we ascend a steep, winding driveway. I see several small buildings. We stop at the one marked "Main Office." I have never been to Stone Gates. I had only seen one small picture on the Internet when I looked it up.

The name is Stone Gates Psychiatric Hospital. This is where I am going. I am not crazy, I swear.

CHAPTER THREE

"WAIT HERE," MY MOTHER SAYS AS SHE PUTS THE CAR IN PARK AND turns it off. I wonder if she notices that I see she takes the keys with her. What does she think? That I will steal the car, so I do not have to come here? Or maybe it is just habit. She did catch me taking the car out after curfew on more than one occasion. I always seemed to have an excuse, though. I am not sure it was a good excuse, but my mother always accepted my excuse without any consequence. Like I said, she is a lot less strict than most parents would be. But now here we are. My actions have left her no other choice. I know she thinks this is what is best. Perhaps a part of me agrees. So, I have come willingly. That does not mean I have to be completely happy about it, though. As I wait for my mother in the car now, I feel myself growing anxious. I cannot see her from where I sit in the car.

Finally, when I feel I can no longer bear it and contemplate going in after her, my mother emerges from the building. Beside her is a tall woman with plain features and brown hair pulled back into a neat bun.

My mother opens the door, and the woman introduces herself to me. "Hello, Katrina. I am Kelly. I have been waiting for your arrival. I am going to bring you to your cabin, Cabin C, and I will help you get settled in."

"Sure" is all I say. I am not trying to be rude, but I have grown anxious. It feels like, all at once, it has hit me. My mother will be leaving soon...without me. I offer a half smile. She seems nice, and, after all, it is not her fault my life has become so completely screwed up.

"It is just over there." The woman...Kelly...points to the left of where the car is parked. "We can walk from here."

I nod my head this time and step out of the car. A medium-sized duffel bag and backpack is all I have brought with me. Kelly takes my duffel bag. This makes me like her just a little. Perhaps this place will not be so bad after all.

As we begin to walk, my mother asks various questions about schedule and therapy. Yup, I knew that was coming. Just before we reach the five steps to Cabin C, my cabin and new home for now, my mother asks one of those questions that I had been dreading. "Kelly, what are the policies on visitation?" She is trying not to show that she is concerned with the answer to this question. But I know better.

Kelly smiles with sympathy; obviously she can read how my mother is feeling as well. Or maybe she has just met a dozen mothers like her. Mothers whose children made bad choices without any obvious rhyme or reason. "We have found that the most progress is made with no visits in the beginning, just to allow the child, even at the age of seventeen to get settled and sort through their own thoughts and emotions. Generally, two weeks is asked of no visits. Then after that we require group therapy once a week when we ask family to come. However, if she settles in nicely, more regular visits can be done. You can even come have dinner with her. You may not think so, but the food here is actually very good." Kelly chuckles at this, trying to lighten the mood. We are now going up the stairs.

"No visits for two weeks?" Both women turn to look at me, and it takes me a minute to realize I have spoken this out loud.

CHAPTER FOUR

Both women's faces soften as they look at me. It is the first time I have seen my mother's face ease from its hard and rigid lines of stress when looking at me in a while. Still, she seems at a loss for words. Kelly more prepared for these types of situations I am sure, smiles warmly at me. It is in this moment I decide I will try, try my very best to trust this woman I have just met.

"Come on," she says. "How about we get you settled, and then the three of us can sit and talk before your mother has to leave? Maybe we could get some dinner?" Kelly looks expectantly first at me and then at my mother. Both of us hesitate to answer. "I meant what I said. The food is really good here." Kelly smiled.

The softness from my mother's face dissolves, and in its place, sadness and defeat take place. "That would be fine."

I say nothing, which both women seem to take as a yes. We continue inside with Kelly leading the way. As we enter the very white walls of the building, a woman's voice seems to vibrate the entire room.

"This is unacceptable!" she shouts. "How is my son supposed to get better and concentrate on his health when you people are rooming him with trollops!"

The air seems to disappear right out of the room as jaws drop.

CHAPTER FIVE

All at the same time, multiple responses emanate around what now seems like a very small space. I feel in myself a shrinking feeling, willing myself to disappear from this confrontation that is brewing before me. My mother's eyes are wide in what appears to be both astonishment and panic as I can practically feel her second-guess this place that she had decided weeks ago was the solution for her daughter, a last and only hope. Kelly remains stoic, waiting in anticipation to see how her fellow colleague will respond to the tall, thin woman. The woman is dressed up as if she is attending a board meeting, not a psychiatric hospital. Her face is a deep red I am sure I have not even seen on my own mother's face. My mother, whose eyes are still wide in anticipation, waits for the woman's response. The woman stands about a foot shorter than her with a lot more meat on her bones, not chunky, but quite thick.

"Ma'am, I can assure you that even though the girls and boys are in the same building, they sleep in separate quarters. There is also a person posted around the clock to make sure they stay in these separate quarters. Windows are permanently sealed in all bedrooms, so the only way out is past said person keeping post. The children are under twenty-four-hour supervision and have schedules they keep, as well as chores that all earn them points. The better they do, the more privileges they have. I can assure you this is a system that works and has done so for many years," the woman says all this as if she has had to explain this to multiple parents over the years. It sounds like she had anticipated the well-dressed women's next three questions, leaving the well-dressed woman silent at last.

Although the woman does not seem to have a response on hand, she still does not seem happy. To add fuel to fire, my own mother has been hanging on every word, and she now seems equally upset. It is then that my mother steps forward to stand beside the slender woman and approach the other, and I brace myself for what comes next.

CHAPTER SIX

"Excuse me," my mother says. "I am hearing this right? Girls and boys are in the same building? So instead of worrying about my daughter sneaking out...you are basically bringing the boys right to her?"

This fuels up the other woman once again. "This is exactly what I am talking about! My son does not need this sort of girl around him when he is trying to better his health!"

My mother snaps her head from the shorter woman in front of her to the tall, slender one that stands beside her. If there was any hope of these two women joining forces on a common ground, that hope has completely evaporated, and ice daggers have cut through any camaraderie.

"Pardon me, lady," my mother snaps at the woman. "You do not even know my daughter. How dare you speak about her! I am sure your son is not so innocent. He is a guy after all, and they only want one thing!"

My mother's face now burns almost as red as the other woman's face. I do not think I have ever seen her get this mad, not even at me, not even with all I have done these past couple of months. I stare in shock at both women—my mother, who has been through so much, who I have put through so much, and then this other woman, who I have known for less than five minutes, and I really know nothing about except the fact that she is tall, thin, and well-dressed. Oh, and she has a son. Wait...

It is only then I notice a boy who looks to be about my age sitting on a chair nearby. He appears tall and thin like his mother, though he is slumped in the chair, so it is hard to tell. Now that I have noticed him, it is hard to tear my eyes away, and the adults have faded into the background. I am not hearing their words anymore, only noticing this boy and wondering what his story is. He is the first person I have come across who is my age since my arrival. I study him, really taking him in. After a closer look I notice that, although he is thin like his mom, his shoulders are broad. They are not huge, but they have definition, as do his arms. The white T-shirt he wears pulls at his muscles, stretching out the material just a little. I am guessing he is into athletics of some kind. He is not quite big enough for football...but maybe baseball or basketball. His hair is light brown and straight like his mother's. It is cut short with just enough length to it on the top to fall over his eyes with his head tilted. A dark blue cap sits on top of his head with his hair spilling out in a way that makes him seem both innocent and intriguing at the same time.

As if reading my thoughts, the boy looked up just then, revealing the most jade green eyes I have ever seen. Something in them is so sad it sends a shiver straight through my entire body, right to my very core.

CHAPTER SEVEN

I WONDER AS I LOOK INTO THOSE SAD GREEN EYES IF THAT IS WHAT people see when they look at me. Is that what this boy is seeing right now? I then realize that I am indeed staring. The boy seems to realize this as well and in response he quickly lowers his head once again. His mother is now in the office with the shorter lady. She looks as if she had calmed down some, at the very least she is no longer yelling. I look around for my own mother. She is talking to Kelly. They speak in hushed tones. Now that I have come back to reality and have stopped staring at the boy, I try to hear what they are saying. Either they do not want to be loud and talk with the boy still sitting out here, or they do not want me to hear. I am thinking the latter.

Well, this is my life too, and that is just not going to fly with me. I walk over to the two women.

"Is there a problem?" I ask, looking pointedly at both women. Yup, and there goes my attitude. I usually am a good kid at least I was before this summer. I mean, yeah, I drink and smoke pot sometimes. But those are typical teenage things, right? I get decent grades and did cheerleading up until my senior year when I started focusing on college and working more hours to pay for said college.

I may not be an angel, but I am a pretty good kid. Or at least I was. However, my attitude...that has always been my downfall.

"No, there is no problem, Kat. Please check the attitude," my mother responds, sighing.

I debate whether to press her. After a moment I decide to leave it alone, for now at least. I also let go of the fact that my mother is the only person on Earth still allowed to call me Kat. That is an argument for another day as well.

"Since the office that has the proper paperwork to register you is occupied, why don't I show you to your room?" Kelly offers. "We can put your bags down, and I'll show you around. After I have shown you around, we can get just a short amount of paperwork out of the way. Then we can go get dinner."

My mother and I both nod in agreement. We follow Kelly up yet another flight of stairs. But something follows me up as we make our way to my new room: the image of that boy. I do not know why I cannot shake those sad eyes or the feeling they give me. I do know one thing though, and that is I do not like it. I do not like it at all.

CHAPTER EIGHT

As we reach the top of the stairs, we come to a long corridor with three doors on each side. Kelly shows us to the last door on the right side. "This will be your room," Kelly says as she opens the door. Standing inside is a girl not much taller than me with jet-black hair. Her eyes look just as black, especially with all the makeup.

My mother is the first to speak. "I did not realize the rooms were shared."

"All the rooms accommodate two people in this section. Most are like this, aside from some special circumstances," Kelly explains.

"She means the rich people who do not have to rely on insurance to pay for their little fucked-up children to be here." The girl says this with a completely straight face, lacking any emotion at all.

"Language, Nia. That will be one demerit," Kelly says sternly. Okay, so she can be tough when she wants to be. The girl just cursed, not a huge deal in my book. Not that I am going to jump in and defend this girl. I do not know her, and I doubt she wants to get to know me. Kelly turns to me then and says, "This is Nia, your roommate." She then turns back to Nia. "Nia, this is Katrina. I expect you will make her feel welcome."

"Hey" is all I say. This girl does not seem like the welcoming type.

Nia just nods at me and turns on her heels to sit on her bed. She picks up a book and begins to read. From where I am standing, I see she is reading *The Silence of the Lambs* by Thomas Harris. I have never read the book, but I did see the movie on television. It is about a psychotic killer. Great, not only is this girl not that friendly, but I will most likely be lucky if she does not stab me in my sleep. I wonder both if I should worry about this girl, and how in the world did she get that reading material approved in a place like this? I do not dare ask this out loud, however. I do not want to draw attention to myself in front of my new roommate, nor do I want to offend her. Perhaps it pertains to her studies, or there is another perfectly logical explanation. After all, I am in no position to judge giving my current status-que in life.

CHAPTER NINE

KELLY BRIEFLY SHOWS ME AROUND THE ROOM. THERE IS NOT MUCH to show. Two beds, two small closets, and two small dressers. We are not allowed to hang anything on the wall. We are allowed personal items, but they must be approved. I mean *everything* must to be approved. Everything from our clothes to photos and even music we play either in a CD player or iPod, whichever we may have brought from home. We are only allowed to listen to the music of our choice through earbuds so no one else can hear. However, I am told by Kelly that they play music of the staff's choice in the rec room downstairs, to which Nia says a brief "huh," never tearing her eyes away from the book.

The worst of it all, though? No phones! We are not allowed to keep our cell phones. Not even for the pictures. I had looked at my mother when Kelly informed us of this, and my mother just shrugged apologetically. I suppose my mother did not realize this either, it would not have been a question she would have thought to ask considering she barely knows how to use her own cell phone. I would have asked had I been given the chance. However, I was not asked much of anything concerning this decision. Though, even if I will not admit it out loud, I do know I need help, and this seems to be the place to get it. But they sure do have a lot of rules. Am I coming here to get help, or is this a jail sentence? I am beginning to wonder. I have been informed that we get monitored phone time. We start out with one hour a week, and, depending on our points or demerits, we can increase or decrease our phone time.

"Everything is earned," Kelly says. "This is your first week here, Katrina. We do not expect you to get it all this week. We do allow the first week for you to adjust. But after that we will expect you to be working on yourself. That is why you are here, right?" She gives me a half smile as if to soften the blow that I am stuck in this place whether I like it or not.

"Sure" is all I say. I see my mother gesture as if to say something, but then she stops herself and remains silent. She is trying to let Kelly run the show now. I see her pulling back. I see how heavy her eyes look. I know it is my fault. But the shame I feel does not allow me to explain to my mother how sorry I am. I suppose this place will make me face that soon enough.

CHAPTER TEN

We sit in the large dining hall now and I move the pasta around my plate, already having picked out all the chicken. Kelly was right about one thing: the food here is amazing. Chicken Florentine is also one of my favorite meals. However, as per usual these days, I am just not that hungry.

Kelly and my mom are talking now about policies, procedures, and such. I am only half paying attention as I push my food around my plate, trying to make myself eat more. We had left the room without another word from my ray of sunshine roommate, and by the time we got downstairs, the boy with the haunting eyes and his semi-scary mother were nowhere to be seen.

Thankfully, Kelly had also been telling the truth about the paperwork not taking too long. My mother had done the brunt of it online when she had first found the place. It had only been the second one she had looked at. It was a little further than the other, but she got a "good feeling" about this place, she had said. I, however, was still not so sure. I was especially not so sure with all these rules and regulations they had. I was not the biggest rebel, but that was with a forgiving mother when I broke curfew on a constant basis. I had a feeling these people would not be so forgiving.

I have now completely tuned out the two women who sit by me, my mother across me and Kelly to my left. The door to the cafeteria lies to my right. I aimlessly look in its direction as I imagine what my life is going to look like in this place. Then I see him. His hat is no longer on his head, and a green and white button-up shirt hides his defined muscles more than the T-shirt had, but it is the boy from when I had first arrived. Mr. Sad Eyes himself. Only his eyes do not look so sad; they look an even brighter jade green than earlier. Not only are they the most piercing green eyes I have ever seen, but they are looking right at me.

CHAPTER ELEVEN

THE BOY DOES NOT HOLD MY STARE FOR LONG, BUT IT IS LONG enough. What is this feeling I get with this guy? I feel both sad and intrigued. I feel like I want to get as far away from this boy as possible, but I want to know everything about him. It must be because I saw his mother in action. That must be the reason. I mean, I have had crushes before and checked guys out plenty. I am a teenage girl, after all. This is different, even though I cannot deny he is one of the most handsome guys I have ever seen off the television screen, maybe even the most handsome guy I have laid eyes on at all. No, this is not a crush. I just feel like maybe this boy has been through something that I could not take on in addition to my own lurking problems. But at the same time, I want to help him through whatever it is he is going through. But that is crazy. Why would I want to help someone who is a total stranger?

He saw me. I know he did. I do not think he was checking me out, though. But then, I was never good at telling these things, as Alyssa liked to point out all too often. My best friend in the whole word—she is more outgoing than I am, but other than that we are a lot alike. We were kind of rebels, but not really. Only Alyssa's parents are still happily married, and she has more money. Not rich, but damn close. I push Alyssa out of my mind. I do not want to think about her and her betrayal right now.

I search for the boy again. If anything, this boy, and his mysteries give me something else to focus on than myself and my current situation. He is on the food line getting food now. I wonder if his mother will be joining him. I look around in search for her. Nope, no sign of her.

"Hello, Kat." My mother waves her hand in front of my face. "Just who in the world are you looking for?" She looks at me with worry and question.

"I am not looking for anyone Mom. I was just looking. I was just taking in my new surroundings." I focus on her now as every fiber in my body must fight the urge to search for the boy.

"Well, it is time I get going. So can I walk you back to your room?" My mother looks at me. She seems to be trying to have a brave face.

I decide I am not going to make it quite so easy for her. "My room is back in Indian Lake. You know, our home that you will be going back to shortly," I say, but without conviction. I get up then and walk to the exit to wait for the two women, one my mother, the other a total stranger. I am eager to get away from them, however I would feel like an even bigger shit if I did not say goodbye to my mom. So, I wait. As I stand by the exit, I cannot help myself. I search for the boy. I cannot find him anywhere. Disappointment creeps into the pit of my gut like an aching that feels heavy inside my stomach. Suddenly I need to see him. I need the distraction.

CHAPTER TWELVE

THE THREE OF US, ME AND THESE TWO ADULT WOMEN WHO HAVE more say over my life than I do, walk back to the cabin in silence. My things are in my room but still need to be unpacked. Kelly informs me that I can unpack and settle in for the night. Tomorrow we will meet at nine o'clock sharp to go over my schedule for the week. Breakfast, I am informed, is from seven until nine. If we do not get it within those two hours, we then need to wait for lunch, which is twelve to two. However, I am assured, as we get privileges, and will be allowed to have food in the cabin that we may cook in the kitchen downstairs by the rec room during lights on hours. *Great*, I think sarcastically. *Something I can look forward to*.

It does not matter anyway. I have not been eating much all summer. Maybe I will just let myself fade away, and with that, all my problems will too. I feel that same thing I do so often, too often. It is an argument within myself. There is the Kat who wants to give up on everything. To just let it go. To forget the past and give up on eating, dressing, school, all of it. I want to give up on any type of future. Once upon a time, I had wanted to work with children, to be a preschool teacher. But it is clear to me that is not going to be in my future. It is clear to this Kat that she has no future.

Then there is the other Kat. The one that says, *Are you stupid? You are just going to give up? You are going to let what happened to you months ago define you?* Of course, I never speak of the incident that set my current path in motion. Not to anyone. Not to my mom, my aunt, my best friend, or even myself. I will not even let myself think it. But still, this other Kat argues that I will get past this. That I should not give up. That one day it will be a distant memory and it will not define who I am.

The trouble is, I have no idea who to listen to. I watch the life deflate from my mother now. She says goodbye down in the hall instead of walking me up to my room. Not that I can blame her. Why allow me another moment to make her feel guilty, especially when she has no idea why her daughter has been so different? Sure, she knows I am no angel. But I was never this, whatever this is.

As I climb the stairs to my room, I wonder who, exactly, I am. Who is Katrina Rogers? Whoever she is, could you help me find her, because I think she is lost. Or maybe I never really knew her. Maybe life is just a lie. I know one thing, and that is I will have to stop lying and face myself. But what if I do not like that girl? What if I do not like the real Kat? A whisper creeps in my head now, a sadistic whisper. I hear it call to me, *Kitty Kat.*

CHAPTER THIRTEEN

My eyes shoot open so fast I feel a twinge of pain shooting behind my eye socket. My mouth is dry, but my forehead and neck are soaked with sweat. I look around in a daze, bringing my hand to my forehead. When did I fall asleep? I must have walked right into the room and collapsed on top of the bed. My things sit piled by my dresser, untouched. Thankfully, my roommate is not in the room right now. I look at the clock. It is ten minutes after eight. I had passed out for about two hours. Somehow, *he* had found his way into my head.

Is that what this place is going to be about? A constant battle complete with bad dreams? I shake my head, shaking away my dream and trying to clear my head. Just then Nia walks back into the room. She glances my way, but I only lower my head, trying to hide the fact that I had just had a mini breakdown.

From my hooded eyes, I see Nia roll her eyes and sit on her bed, picking up her book and beginning to read once again. I glance her way and notice she has a ton of books on her dresser. Among them, I can see *The Great Pretender, Shades of Blue,* and *The Upside of Being Down.* What is with this girl? That is some depressing reading material. Of course, I have not actually read any of these books, but I am sort of familiar with them. Then I think of the one book I brought with me, *Little Girl Lost* by Drew Barrymore, and Todd Gold. Maybe I should not be so quick to judge.

Suddenly I need to be out of this room. I make my way to the communal bathroom to splash my face and collect myself. I do not even look at my reflection. I cannot stand the sight of myself anymore. Lucky for me, I have clear skin and low maintenance hair these days, the upside of not eating fast food all summer and chopping off my hair. I have also not had a drink in a few weeks, not since the night my mother had decided I needed help beyond what she could give to me. I have been on lockdown since that night. Not that it matters. I do not really have any friends anymore. I have not even talked to Alyssa in weeks. We have been best friends since the first grade, and this is the longest since then that we have gone without talking.

I have nobody except my own thoughts. That is just too scary for me to accept right now. I decide as a distraction to wander around my new surroundings. I cannot leave the cabin at this time. But why not check out the rec room? I am not exactly even sure what is in a rec room. I have heard of houses having a rec room, but certainly not the tiny apartment my mother and I live in.

I pad down the stairs slowly and cautiously. Slowly I make my way to the office. "Umm, excuse me," I say softly. "I am just going to check out the rec room."

It is the same woman who had been here when I had first arrived. She smiles at me now, nothing like the demeanor when I had seen her for the first time. "Of course, you can, darling. But remember, lights out at ten o'clock sharp."

I smile and nod. Turning on my heels sharply, I crash right into a solid, much taller body.

CHAPTER FOURTEEN

I STAND FROZEN FOR JUST A SECOND, FACING A BROAD CHEST. IT ONLY takes me about another second to recognize the green and white button-up shirt. Then I do it. I look up. His hat is back on, shading his face, but I look right into them, those jade green eyes. *Just act casual*, Kat, I tell myself.

"Sorry." I smile, wink, and walk away, heading up to my room. The rec room will have to wait. I am going to die of humiliation now. Why the hell did I wink at him? Sometimes I feel as if my body is taken over when it comes to boys. I have always played hard to get, or, as the boys in my school would call me, a tease. But I do not care what they thought. College was going to be where I would start to take guys seriously, not cheesy high school boys. But I guess that plan has changed now too.

As I reach the stairs, I look up to see my roommate, Nia, coming down the stairs. Of course, she has seen the whole thing. "Nice one, roomie," she says as she passes me. Then she makes her way right over to Mr. Green Eyes. "You will have to forgive my roommate. She can be a bit clumsy. My name is Nia. You just get here today?"

I am walking slowly up the stairs now, hanging onto the conversation I left behind. She is flirting with him! I bet she is not even interested in him and is doing this just to get to me. Why did I not stick around to talk to him? I groan in my head to myself. What do I even care, right? What do I think? That we had some epic love connection just because our eyes had locked a few times? It has been three times they have locked now, but who is counting, right? Well, three times including this last time when I basically bolted away. The other two times, he had looked away. What do I think—I was going to find some ultimate romance in here, a place of literal wall-to-wall issues and the people who carry them like old baggage? I mean, that is basically what this is, wall-to-wall issues, each more messed up than the next, I guess. Perhaps I am wrong, though. Perhaps I am the most messed up out of this whole lot of fouled-up teens to dwell this place. This is just too tragic a concept for me to even entertain. I need a distraction...and this guy is a handsome one at that.

My feet will not carry me to my room until I hear him speak. When he does, I know I am doomed because those eyes are paired with something much more dangerous. In the most deep, silky smooth English accent I have ever heard in my life, I hear him say, "Name is Scott. Yes, I arrived today." No guy that gorgeous has the right to sound so sexy too. I am doomed.

CHAPTER FIFTEEN

My knees grow weak and my stomach queasy. What is happening to me? It is just a voice, Kat. Get a hold of yourself. Perhaps it is the whole situation. I mean, I literally ran right into him and then my not-so-friendly new roommate goes and talks to him. Somehow, I get myself back to my room even though I am feeling panicked suddenly, and I do not know why. To distract myself from my awkward encounter, I begin to put my things away, trying to push all thoughts of Mr.—Well, I guess I could call him Scott now, instead of Mr. Green Eyes—out of my head. Why am I even thinking of him at all? A derailment from what is currently my life in this moment of course is the simple answer. Anything is better than my reality right now.

I finish unpacking quickly, being that there is not much to unpack. I decide to go to bed early. It is a better choice than facing my new roommate, who I am sure cannot wait to rub my encounter in my face based on the way she practically pounced on him as I went sulking to my room.

I must face it. I am in a new place, and there is not a friendly face in sight. Back home I was the bad/good girl. I was friendly with most people but left the real socializing to my best friend, Alyssa. I was not afraid to party but never did anything too crazy. Of course, in the land of teenagers, not being too crazy in many cases also meant not being easy when it came to guys. I would drink and flirt, but when it came down to it, I almost never went through with anything at all. Unfortunately, this also gave me a bit of a reputation as a tease. But I've known most of the guys I went to school with since elementary school, and they did not care much. I was a good drinking buddy, and between Alyssa and me, we always could hunt down the best weed to bring to the party.

I will say the good girl part of me would not let myself drink during the week. Sure, sometimes I would be out after curfew, but I never got wasted during the week. I was just usually hanging out in a parking lot and saved the real partying for the weekend. I thought it was a good balance. I thought I had it all under control. I thought I was just doing typical teenaged things. But I thought wrong. I learned my lesson when a new boy I did not know since elementary school stepped into my life, and he tore it to pieces.

Grant Jessup.

I slip into darkness with that name on my tongue and burning in my brain. Then it comes, the hot sting of tears. Why? Why did this person have to come into my life senior year? I was done. I had one foot out the door and off to college. But now...now my life is in ruins and my heart aches for that girl that I thought I once was. Who is Kat?

Kitty Kat...that awful sadistic voice mocks me as hot tears soak my pillow.

CHAPTER SIXTEEN

I WAKE, FEELING THE STRAIN AND ACHE IN EYES THAT HAVE BEEN CRYING a good part of the night. My mind is fuzzy from the dreams I fought to keep at bay. Fuck, I am still in this foreign place. I lean on my elbows, willing my eyes to work and my head to clear. I notice my roommate's bed is empty and has been made already. Making our bed and keeping the room clean are part of earning points to get privileges around here. It appears my roommate does care after all, at least enough to make her bed. Maybe she has someone she wishes to make a phone call to. It is at this exact moment I realize that I do not. I do not have anyone I wish to make a phone call to—well, maybe my mom. I pinch the bridge of my nose and squeeze my eyes shut tightly. I take in a breath and hold it there.

I need to fix this. I need to fix my life. Of course, I feel this way now, but I am sure in no time I will want to give up again. I glance at the clock. 8:42 a.m. Well, I never really did care for breakfast anyway. But I do still have to meet with Kelly at nine.

I drag my body out of bed to get ready. It feels like lead, and my stomach feels as if it has rocks rolling around in it. Well, here we go…either this will be my new beginning or the beginning of the end for me. I make my way downstairs, my black sweatpants feeling looser than usual as I walk. I just do not feel the need to put effort into my appearance these days. With my black sweatpants, I chose a black tank top as well. Dark colors for a dark day. Then I laugh to myself. I really laugh out loud. My whole entire wardrobe is basically black. Sure, I have some blues and army greens in there, but all dark. When did this happen? When did I close out the light?

"What is so funny? Did you crash into someone else?" I am greeted with that accent...that accent and...a smile?

"Oh...umm...yeah, sorry about that." I am at a loss for words. What the hell is happening to me? I never lose my words like this around some guy, some guy I do not even know and once I have left here will never see again in my life, no less.

"No worries, love," he says. Today he wears another white T-shirt and khaki pants. He looks incredible. He appears so good and pure. It is making me feel a certain way that I do not recognize, and I both love it and hate it at the same time.

It takes all I have, but I gather my composure. "My name is Katrina." I smile back at him.

"Oh, I did not mean any offense. I call everyone love," he defends himself.

I giggle. He is adorable, and I bet he does not even realize the trouble he could be. "I know...I have seen an English movie or two. I was just letting you know my name. The least I can do after bumping into you, I suppose." I continue to smile back at him. I could almost swear I see him blush.

"I am Scott, nice to meet you, Katrina."

With that, I silently love him for not calling me Kat.

CHAPTER NINETEEN

WELL, I GUESS MY PLAN WORKED. SCOTT DOES SEEM TO WANT MORE, or I have completely freaked him out and he is deciding if he should be scared or not. Really, I am sure it could go either way. Because right now, I can literally feel his eyes burning into me as I sit by myself in the dining hall.

"Hey, I'm Jazzie, mind if I sit?" It is the blond girl from earlier. Why not? I could use at least one friend in this place.

"Sure, why not." I smile at Jazzie, but it is an empty smile because my mind is swimming with so many thoughts right now that I cannot focus on anything.

"What? Do not tell me you are second guessing that move you pulled earlier...because that was awesome. Trust me, I am a bold person, and I never even did anything like that."

"Yeah, well, playing guys like an instrument is kind of my thing. Only, I think I really like this guy. Which is crazy, but, I mean, I am probably crazy...or slowly getting there anyway. I mean, I am here." I give a little laugh. It does not come from my belly, but I try.

"Are you trying to say that I am crazy?" Suddenly, Jazzie looks serious. I sit, stuck. Shit. I mean, I can probably take her, but I did not mean to offend her. I could really use a friend in this place. I am just not thinking clearly. This is what this guy is doing to me. Or maybe I am doing it to myself. I sat in silence, waiting for some indication if I was going to have to throw down in the middle of this dining hall. Oh no, I hoped not in from of *him*. I begin to become nervous, and it must show.

"Relax, I am messing with you. Sorry, that is kind of my thing. I am unforgivingly sarcastic at times, but you will get used to it." Jazzie fixes me with a toothy smile, and she digs into her brown rice and shoves a huge spoonful into her mouth.

Then I do it. I laugh, out loud and from deep within my belly. I have not laughed, not really laughed like that...well, I can't remember the last time. Not like this. No, this is a real laugh, like the kind that friends share when one tells a joke or says something witty that only their friend gets. That is when I know. I know this girl and I are going to be friends.

"You know," Jazzie whispers as she finishes the last bite of her rice. "I heard your boy is a virgin."

"What, a guy that age? No way," I protest as I push my rice round on my still-full plate. I have taken a total of three bites. I am used to forcing back at least three bites because this is what my mother asks of me. I figure I should stick to the three bites, so I do not get sick. I have already fainted once. I think my mother had about twenty more gray hairs when I came to my senses. I do not want to do that again, even if my mother is miles away. I am sure this place will be reporting everything back to her.

"My roommate, she is kind of lame, but somehow that girl always finds out the gossip. Her name is Jen. She said this guy's mom is strict, does not let him date."

"Oh." This is all I say.

"What? Do you know something? You just got quiet."

"Well, I met his mother when I got here. That does make a lot of sense."

"Hey, maybe you could pop his cherry, huh?" Jazzie says, raising her eyebrows.

Jazz and I both burst out laughing. That is when we round the corner and straight into Nia, my ever-charming roommate. "Hey, watch it!" she snaps. Then she takes a good look at who has just run into her path. "Well, look at this. The troll found a friend."

"Nia, you are so beautiful. Who does your makeup?" Jazz says this with a wicked grin. "A makeup artist whose specialty is applying makeup to clowns from the local circus?"

"Do not worry. When you are big enough, maybe you can wear makeup too," Nia returns just as wickedly.

What have I gotten myself in the middle of here?

CHAPTER TWENTY

"WHOA, WHAT WAS THAT ABOUT?" I ASK JAZZIE, MY DARK BROWN eyes burning into her crystal blue ones.

"What? Nia?" she asks, all casual, as if it was just business as usual.

"Yeah Nia, that is my roommate."

"Oh, damn, girl, I would start sleeping with a weapon under my pillow."

My mouth falls open in shock.

"I am kidding!" says Jazzie. "That girl's bark is worse than her bite. We went to the same school. We are kind of friendenemies, you could say. So, when the two of us both ended up here, Nia figured it was the perfect chance to torture me."

"Oh" is all I say.

"Look, she is fairly harmless. However, now that she knows you are friends with me, I would not expect her to be nice to you anytime soon. We have just never really liked each other. No major story there, just two different people."

I look at Jazzie suspiciously, feeling like I am not getting the whole story. Finally, Jazzie relents. "Okay," she says, throwing her hands up in the air. "I may have slept with her boyfriend...like the only guy she ever dated in our school...while they were together."

"Damn, girl." This is all I say to Jazzie.

"I guess I should also mention at this time that word is she was checking out your boy. If you are really into this guy, I would make a move quick. Before ice queen sinks her claws into him. Because once she does, trust me, you are not going to want to look in his direction."

CHAPTER TWENTY-ONE

As I lie in bed, a storm of thoughts swirl around in my head like a cyclone. Jazzie's words repeat in my head, and I wonder just how intimated of Nia I should be. I wonder if this guy is worth making a move on, and if I am even ready if he does show interest. Could I take it beyond being a tease? Could I ever see myself having a relationship? I mean, it did not exactly work out for my mom. What if being a failure at a relationship was genetic? I have never even seen my mom on a date, not for the entire time I was growing up. It was always just me and her. Now it feels more like it is just me.

I glance over at Nia as she lies sleeping. Sleep is seemingly a stranger for me in this moment. I do not know much about this girl. One fact I do know is she never said anything to me about having an interest in Scott. It could even just be a rumor. Who is to say that he would be interested in her as well, anyway? Who is to say he would be interested in me? I know from the reactions I have gotten from guys I am not horrible looking...but, let's face it, I have issues. Even I can admit that much.

Still, I cannot help this pull I feel toward Scott. Why have I never felt this before, and why is it happening now? I can hear his voice now, saying my name. I can feel it covering me like a velvet blanket.

In that moment I decide. I decide that tomorrow, no matter what, I am going to make my move on Scott. Now all I need to do was to think of a plan. I need to get him alone for this. But, how, when and where was the question. I have a lot to figure out, it seems...and my other looming issues would have to wait. This...this will be my current priority. The drama that is my life, those demons that hover over me at night—well, that would have to wait.

CHAPTER TWENTY-TWO

As if fate has suddenly decided that maybe it is not such a good idea if Scott and I are thrown together, I have not seen him all day. It is not like this place is that big. Where could he be? My stomach turns. Tomorrow I have my first therapy session, the first real one after the introduction session I had already, and I desperately need a distraction.

I just left Jazzie, who said she has not seen him either. As I departed from Jazzie, in usual Jazzie style, she had turned to me with a sly smile and said, "Oh, and Katrina...tick tock."

"Thank you for your support." I had rolled my eyes. It is strange to have this new person in my life. I feel instantly comfortable with her. This is unusual for me to trust so easily. However, she is not going to be gentle or tiptoe around my feelings. This is what I like about her most. It seems people who know me are either afraid to say things about me or they are just fake. With Jazzie, I feel like she tells it like it is.

With that extra push, I decide to try my luck at the rec room. After all, I had found him there before. But no luck, his was not there. The rec room is empty. I pad over to the books; maybe a good story could be a viable distraction. I spot *The Outsiders* by S. E. Hinton. Score! What a classic story, and not a romance. It was perfect.

I settle myself on a chair with the book and immerse myself in it immediately. I do not want to retreat to my room just yet. I do not want to face Nia yet. I still cannot make up my mind about that girl. She is not exactly friendly, but I still cannot determine her bite compared to her bark. Personally, I am more of a lover than a fighter, but if I need to bite back and involve myself in a fight, I will and have had to on an occasion or two. Usually, with boys...

I let my thoughts fade away as I read about Pony Boy stepping out of that movie theater and into an adventure he had not bargained for. I lose all sense of time and am well into chapter five where the boys are already holed up in the church when I hear a voice. It is not just any voice, though...it is that smooth, velvety English accent... and I did not expect it. I had not even heard anyone come into the rec room. So, I do what any rational person would do...I scream.

CHAPTER TWENTY-THREE

I IMMEDIATELY REGRET MY REACTION AS I HEAR FOOTSTEPS COMING toward the rec room. Kelly bursts in, panic clearly on her face.

"I am so sorry, Kelly," I say right away. "I was so involved in my book I did not hear Scott enter the room. I just got startled, not a big deal."

"Are you okay?" The way Kelly asks this is as if she knows that I have a reason to be startled so easily. As if she knows that secret that I have been holding deep inside, deep in that part of the brain that will not even allow me to admit the truth. But she could not know... could she?!

"I am fine. I said that already." I drop the book suddenly without even saving the page I had been reading only moments ago. Was I not going to get enough inquiry tomorrow? "I am going to get some air before curfew."

I walk straight out of the building without looking at either Kelly or Scott. I make my way to the smoking section. I had quit the same time I had stopped drinking. I had never liked it all that much anyway, not as much as I enjoyed drinking. I just did it to pass the time. It was better than having to talk around a bunch of people that I could feel judging me anyway, judging the tease. But now I feel myself craving a cigarette, to feel the burn of the smoke paired with the cool mint of the menthol. Just to feel something physically that would take my mind off all the other thoughts swirling around in my head, threatening to take root, grow, and fester inside.

I debate asking someone for a cigarette, but as I round the corner, no one is there anyway. It is probably for the best. I am sure they would just report that to my mom if I was spotted smoking. When Kelly had mentioned that a permission slip would need to be signed for smoking privileges my mother had been very adamant that I do not smoke and so that would not be necessary. Although, I am almost certain my mother knew full-well that I used to smoke. She most likely thinks that if I did again it would lead straight to drinking and smoking weed again. As if I could get away with that in this place, or could I? I was not willing to chance finding out right now.

I suck in the night air. What the hell am I doing here? I am going to start smoking again and making steps backward? Suddenly, I feel relieved no one was there. *I could still go for a drink though*; I think to myself. No harm in that, right. I mean, even women of sophistication indulged in a glass of wine or two sometimes, right? I think this even though, deep down, I know damn well a liter of vodka and a glass of wine are nowhere near the same thing.

"You dropped this."

Mmm, that voice. This time I do not scream. This time I decide I will "carpe diem," as they say. I am going to seize the day and seize this moment. I finally have my moment alone with Scott, and I am going to make it count.

CHAPTER TWENTY-FOUR

I SLOWLY TURN AROUND TO FACE THOSE RADIANT GREEN EYES. MY eyes lock with Scott's, barely glimpsing at the book he holds in his outstretched hand. I step closer to Scott in one fluid movement. Instantly, I feel his body reacting to mine. I am making him nervous as I draw closer.

"Thank you," I say, my eyes never leaving his as I take the book from his hand and allow my own hand to touch his and linger there. I reach up to his ear and whisper, "It looks like I owe you now... please allow me to start paying you back immediately." I graze my lips along his cheek, slowly reaching his own lips. I press my lips to his hard. My body is now leaning into his.

At first his lips eagerly return my kiss as his tongue finds my own, but just as quickly and feverishly, Scott pulls his body away. The warmth between us dissipates into the air.

"Katrina, we should not do this." he says, his breath heavy and hot, and I want to taste his breath once again and steal it away to savor as my own. I want to feel the warmth of his body and melt into it. "Why don't we sit and talk instead?"

But I do not want to sit and talk. I do not want to think. No, no. I just want to feel. I am not asking for sex here. I have only ever been to third base, anyway. I was a tease after all. Now here I am offering a sample, and he does not even want that much of me. I laugh in my head. Scott must think I have had plenty of sex and I will ruin him.

Suddenly, I grow angry. Does he think I am some skank that will ruin him? I bet that is what he thinks, what his *mommy* has drilled into his head since he was playing in the sandbox with mini versions of girls like me, little girls she deemed unworthy for her son. I want to say this to him right now. Accuse him of thinking me unworthy of him.

However, all I say is, "If I wanted to talk, I would go see my therapist." I begin to walk away...but then I turn back to Scott. "Why did you even follow me out here, anyway?"

I cannot be sure, but I think Scott looks genuinely sad all of a sudden. "Because...because I have seen the look you had when I startled you before, and I thought you could use a friend to talk to."

A lump forms in my throat. How could he? I feel as if everyone is in on my secret, the secret I have been keeping even from myself. Panic sets in, and my defenses go up. "You do not know anything about me. You are not my friend." This time I do not stick around long enough for a reaction.

CHAPTER TWENTY-FIVE

As I lie in bed, I replay the ending of my night over and over. Scott had offered to sit and talk. Why? This is a foreign concept to me. A guy who wants to just talk? Not in my experience. Especially when it came to...well, I refuse to even say his name. Really, it was all men I had come across...well, boys anyway. I do not even know why or how I came to feel this way. It could be that I grew up without a father and no male figure around. Or maybe that is an unfair assumption. What I do know is that the only males I know of were the horny, prepubescent minions at my school. Sure, they were harmless for the most part. However, once they learned I was not as easy as my flirty personality indicated, they basically stayed away from me. Of course, they would drink with me and smoke my weed, though. They were horny, not completely stupid. Not one had ever tried to have a real conversation with me, though, not ever.

I guess I knew Scott was different from the first time I saw his sad eyes hiding under the brim of that hat, though. This is the reason why he got to me. Scott got under my skin. My natural reaction is to flirt. I do not want to be serious. I do not want to *talk*. I just want to feel better. I especially need to with this impending therapy session tomorrow. I want to feel a pure physical connection, not a meeting of the minds.

Thankfully, I do not think anyone saw Scott and me. I do not need any unwanted attention right now to add to my expanding pile of shit I seem to be building all on my own. As I hear the door start to open, I screw my eyes shut tight. I also do not need to deal with Nia right now. As Nia enters the room, she does not even try to be quiet in the least. Finally, after she stomped and rustled a bag that could not possibly have anything left in it and I am sure she was just shaking to annoy me with the noise, I sit up in bed. “Are you about done? I am trying to sleep here.”

Nia turns to me with a sugary-sweet smile. “Oh, did I wake you? I am so sorry. I must not have noticed that I was making so much noise. I am just in such a good mood after my conversation with Scott. Do you know Scott? Hmm, of course you do.”

What is this bitch trying to pull? “What is that supposed to mean,” I demand. “What did he say about me?” I ask, scared he has told her all about how I hit on him only moments ago and how he rejected me.

“Do not flatter yourself, Kat. Your name did not even come up.”

I can’t tell if she is lying, but I really hope she is not, not about this anyway.

However, all I say is “Do not fucking call me Kat. It’s Katrina.”

Nia holds her arms up, palms facing out in mock defense. “Sorry,” she says. But she does not look sorry. She does not look sorry at all.

CHAPTER TWENTY-SIX

As my eyes slowly flutter open, letting in the brightness of the morning sun, for a fleeting moment I forget the events of the night before. Then in a wave, it comes back to me. My scream and Kelly running in, and she seemed to know why I would frighten so easily. Then there was my run-in with Scott and ending the night with his rejection. Oh, and let us not forget Nia's bragging. At least she did not seem to have a clue about my interactions with him that night. Nothing like a silver lining in what was a horrible night and what will surely be an even more horrible of a day to follow.

Today I will start my therapy. I have no idea what to expect. I know in the pit of my stomach I will have to talk about everything, and I mean *everything*, at some point. I just do not know when that point will be. Would Kelly want to dive right into the topic that I am so very much dreading because of last night's events?

It seems like I am my own worst enemy, always making things more difficult. I suck in my breath and roll to my side to check my clock. It is another day that I missed breakfast, oh well. Therapy is at ten today, so I have plenty of time to get ready for that at least. After a semi-hot shower and finally picking out some jeans and a shirt that says "Luke's Diner" on it, I have only fifteen minutes until my therapy session. *I may as well head down*, I think to myself.

Because fate is out to get me, as soon as I reach the bottom of the stairs, my eyes lock with those brilliant green eyes I have been dreading to see. Why would I not have an awkward moment before therapy? I swear, sometimes I can hear someone laughing at me from up above.

Being the "mature adult" that I am, I decide ignoring Scott is the best approach. Of course, pretending not to see him is rather futile because of course he obviously has seen me. As I attempt to walk past Scott, he steps right in front of me. *I do not want to see him*, I tell myself, yet my entire being feels prickly as the electric pull to him courses through my whole body.

"Please, Katrina, can we talk?" his velvety voice asks as he looks at me with pleading eyes. How the hell am I supposed to say no to that voice and those eyes?

"I have therapy" is all I say.

"Could we meet after then?" Scott asks.

"Fine," I say as indifferently as I can muster. Inside, though, I feel even more anxious...but I also feel...hope?

CHAPTER TWENTY-SEVEN

As I cross the threshold into Kelly's office, any glimpse of hope I thought I had feels dissolved, and in its place, I am left with that anxious, achy feeling in the pit of my belly.

"Come in, Katrina. Please have a seat," Kelly greets me with a smile. "You seem nervous. Would you like to start with how you are feeling right now?"

"I guess I am nervous," I say. "I am just not sure what to expect." I try to keep my voice as solemn as I can.

Kelly seems to think for a moment before responding. She then smiles at me warmly and says, "This is an opportunity to help you, and therefore you dictate what happens in these sessions. However, I will remind you that how fast you progress in these sessions also lies with you. It depends on how honest you are both with me and yourself. At this time, I do want to remind you that anything you say here is safe. It will not be shared with anyone, not even your mother and not even in group therapy. Group therapy will be totally separate. In both cases, though, it is the law that I may not share any information from any therapy sessions with anyone at all. Not unless someone is in immediate life-or-death danger. That is the only circumstance I would be allowed to, but anything else is between you and me. I am lawfully obligated to uphold that vow. The vow not to divulge anything you say here. Do you understand? I know it can be a bit much."

Kelly now looks at me expectantly for my response.

"So..." I begin racking my brain. "I could tell you that I kissed a boy while here, and you can't tell my mother, *and* I cannot get in trouble for it?" I wait quite literally on the edge of my seat. Not only am I testing my boundaries, but I really do want to know the answer.

"No, Katrina, I will not and cannot tell your mother. You also cannot get into trouble for telling me this. I want to be totally honest with you, though. Had I seen you kissing a boy, or girl, for that matter, that would be a demerit and would hinder you having privileges. However, I am more interested in why you kissed the boy."

"Well, I did not say that I did. I just wanted to know *what if*," I state to Kelly.

"Remember, Katrina, this cannot work if you are not honest. So, let us say for argument's sake that you did indeed kiss a boy. Why do you think you would do that?"

"Simple, he is hot." I smile at Kelly.

"But, tell me why Katrina? You are here to work on yourself. Tell me why." Kelly pauses, waiting for my response. I am not going to make it that easy for her. I sit quietly, my mouth drawn in a line. I am beginning to dig in my heels.

It seems Kelly is not going to be easy on me either. After all, she is here to do a job, and I am sure just appeasing me is not it. "Why don't you tell me about the boys in your school? Did you kiss any of them, or any you would like to talk about?"

Suddenly my pulse quickens. The last people that I want to talk about are those boys. They are nothing but a waste of space.

Especially...well, I just refuse to do it. My face grows red as I stand up from my seat.

"How dare you!" I spit at Kelly. "I was not talking about those pathetic losers. They are all horrible. I did not want to kiss him...I mean them!" I am screaming now.

Kelly rises to her feet now too. She slowly places one hand on my arm. "Calm down, Katrina. Those boys are not here. They cannot hurt you."

I look at Kelly, hot tears now stinging my eyes. "But he can."

CHAPTER TWENTY-EIGHT

KELLY IS WRONG. HE CAN HURT ME. HE HURTS ME EVERY DAY...AND night, especially at night. Kelly approaches me tentatively now.

"He is not here, Katrina. I know the memory must make it feel like he is...but this guy...he is not here. Do you think you may want to talk about what happened, or tell me his name? Perhaps, if you shared just a little, it would lift a weight off your shoulders."

My tears suddenly stop. I turn my head, so I look right at Kelly, my brow furrowed, and I look at her as if she has just told me the world were flat and the grass were bright pink.

"I will not give him that power...he..." I grit my teeth to the point that it is painful. "He...does not deserve to have his name spoken. He most certainly does not deserve to be spoken about." It seems I have no more tears to spill. "Are we done?"

Kelly seems to deflate in front of me. "Yes, of course, Katrina. We can stop for today. But whether you realize it or not, you did well today. I am proud of you. Actually, I have something for you." Kelly smiles, albeit cautiously.

Is this woman mad? I ask to myself. I think she should be a patient here, because clearly, she has lost it. This is horrible, and why in the world would she be giving me a gift after this shit show?

Kelly walks over to her cabinet and pulls out a notebook. It is brown leather with a tree on the cover etched into the leather material. It is pretty.

"Here." She hands me the notebook. "I want you to write whatever you want in here. You can write fiction or fact, stories, poems, or just thoughts. You can even just draw if you prefer. But this is yours, and no, you do not have to show it to me. It is completely yours and for your eyes only. I just want you to have an outlet. Okay, speech over. You can go."

I nod at Kelly. I simply do not have the energy to do anything else. Then I remember I was supposed to meet Scott after this. That is the last thing I want to do. However, as I exit Kelly's office, there he is, waiting for me. I sigh. Maybe I could use a friend right now. Jazzie is great, but sometimes she can be a bit intense. Perhaps I should try...being friends with a boy? Well, I suppose crazier things happen every day. Suddenly, I grow nervous, though. Did he hear me yelling in there?

I slowly pad over to him.

"How did it go?" he asks, looking sincere about it.

"You mean..." I hesitate. "You did not hear from out here?"

"Hear what?" he asks, and he truly looks like he had no idea what I am talking about.

"Hear me screaming?"

"No. Soundproof, remember?"

I had not remembered, but I am relieved.

"So, what were you screaming about," Scott asks, his eyes studying me in question.

"Oh, no," I say. "If we are going to be friends, we need to set some ground rules."

"Oh, we are friends now?" Scott asks, and he smiles. "Because" he continues, "I had this whole speech planned. I was going to really have at it, really going to work for this friendship. Now you say that is it, we are friends?"

Just like that, my rage dissolves like sugary cotton candy on my tongue. I do not know how, but just standing there with Scott makes me feel safe. I even crack a small smile myself.

"No, I said we need to set some ground rules."

"All right, then. Fancy a walk while we discuss these rules?"

I nod my head. This should be an interesting conversation.

CHAPTER TWENTY-NINE

WE ARE ONLY ALLOWED TO WALK AROUND A CERTAIN PERIMETER, SO Scott and I sit on a bench in front of the building under close supervision. I do not mind the adults watching over us since I have decided being "just friends" with Scott could be a good thing for me. However, the prying eyes of the other kids here feel like an invasion into my very soul. If I knew kids—and people are often predictable—the rumor mill would be buzzing. I sit silently, shifting on the bench awkwardly. Finally, I cannot take the silence as Scott sits just as awkwardly next to me.

"You know, people are probably going to think we are boyfriend and girlfriend just from sitting here together."

"Well," Scott says thoughtfully, "I never did care much about what people thought." He pauses for a good minute while I smile at what he has just said. "And" he continues, "I have never had a girlfriend and I do not intend to, not until I get my life straight at least."

So, the rumors about him had been true. Also, it appears I never had a chance at being more than a friend. I decide at that very moment Scott will indeed be a great friend to have and forget any romantic notions. I will not have to worry about his intentions because they are clear. He does not want a girlfriend. I decide, being a friend, he deserves honesty.

"Well, I have never had a boyfriend."

The look of shock on Scott's face could not be more defined. I mean, he literally drops his jaw. Luckily, I am the only one that notices because the eyes that were on us had already grown bored with us and moved on.

I continue to explain. Scott has been nothing but nice to me. He deserves the whole truth...or most of it, anyway. "I mean, I fooled around with a few guys and gone on dates, or hung out with them in a group, but never had an actual boyfriend."

He looks less surprised.

Katrina goes on to say, "Also I never went all the way. I know you must have thought..."

"I thought nothing," says Scott. "My only thought was that I wished I had your confidence."

"It is an act." I lower my head. It seems I cannot stop the truth from spilling out now.

"Well, I like this version of you better." Just then Scott holds up his hand to shake mine. "Hello, my name is Scott, nice to meet you."

"Katrina." I shake Scott's hand. Even though I can still feel the tingles of electricity, I feel warmth too. There is a calm feeling being around Scott. He is not like any guy I have ever met. *Friends*, Suddenly I like that word.

Scott and I sit and talk for hours about our lives, skipping over the ugliness of what brought each of us here. I decide I do not only want to be his friend, but I need this. He does not ask about what happened, or why I had jumped the other day when he startled me, or any of my awkward moments in between. We talk about family, school, and even hopes for the future. By the end of the week, this becomes a regular routine for us. Sitting and talking, either out front on the bench or in the rec room. Even Jazzie, although in a different cabin close by, joins on the bench. The three of us fall into a routine that feels like a true friendship by the end of the week. We still do not know that much about one another, but we are becoming friends. Conversations become easy, and the three of us even sit together for meals. I even eat a meal or two. I feel lighter...but I find myself still avoiding. All three of us have a nice distraction in our newfound friendship. But that is the thing about demons of the past—they can never stay buried. All three of us will have to deal with our demons at some point or another.

CHAPTER THIRTY

As I head into my second week at Stone Gates, my third therapy session is fast approaching. I never talk about the events that led to me coming to Stone Gates with Jazzie or Scott. I never even allow myself to think them while alone if I can help it. Only at night, when my thoughts cannot be controlled, do I see his face and hear the sadistic call in the dark...*Kitty Kat*. To my great embarrassment, Nia has heard me having my nightmare twice now. I think she's even begun to feel sorry for me because she no longer teases me or even gives me those scowls, I have become used to. The story that Scott is dead set on not having a girlfriend has made its way around. If that is not enough, his mother has visited twice already, clearly not following the two-week rule. No girl wants to deal with that woman, not even Jazzie and me. We steer clear during her visits. Nia has even begun to steer clear of the two of us—losing interest, I suppose. She has moved on to a new boy who arrived just two days ago... Carl, I believe, is his name. They have even sat together at lunch and dinner. Things are calm all around.

I miss my mom, but not seeing her makes me feel less guilty and like the piece of shit I have been feeling like. That will be approaching soon too...my family therapy session is scheduled one week from the third session I have with Kelly tomorrow. At dinner that night as Jazzie and Scott argue over who played the best Batman, I am more quiet than usual. I know they notice my silence, but in this friendship, we do not talk about such things. I still have no idea why either one of them are here. It is an unsaid understanding that we have. They know that I have my session tomorrow. They do not call me out on it, only continue their lighthearted banter. As we exit the dining hall, neither one condemns me for leaving a full plate. I am beginning to cherish their friendship more than they can know. But still, neither one can protect me from what is to come. We each head back to our cabins. Scott and I walk in silence.

I break the silence at last, "listen, I am going to head back to my room early."

"I understand...but I have something to show you tomorrow. Can we meet by the bench after your session?"

"Sure." I smile a half smile before retreating to my room. Well, at least I have a distraction now. What in the world could Scott possibly have to show me?

CHAPTER THIRTY-ONE

All too fast the morning comes. My emotions are more jumbled than ever, like a ball of yarn that has been chased by a cat all day. I dread my session. However, now I cannot help but wonder what in the world Scott must show me. I skip breakfast this morning. If I see Scott, I will just be interrogating him both out of curiosity and as a distraction as to what it is he is going to show me. For all I know, he is not going to show me anything and he only said that as a distraction. Wouldn't that be ironic? I lie in bed until 9:30 a.m.—only a half of an hour more until my therapy session. I finally get up to get ready and drag myself downstairs to Kelly's office.

Inside her office I am surprised to see a giant whiffle ball bat and one of those ugly half mannequins people use in boxing classes. I only know this because Alyssa made me go to one once. Alyssa—I have not spoken to her in so long. Thinking of her, I suddenly feel an ache form in my stomach.

"So, Katrina, what do you think about this guy here?" Kelly asks me as she gives me a smile.

"It makes me think of my best friend, Alyssa. She made me take a boxing class once," I explain, and then I clam up. I have said too much. Damn. I did not want to talk about Alyssa. I cast my eyes down and grow stone-cold silent. Kelly seems to understand.

"Perhaps you could write her a letter in that notebook I gave you. You would not even have to really give it to her. It is something I have done in the past. I wrote a letter to my mom after she passed away."

I look up at Kelly. "You lost your mom? I am sorry." I *am* sorry too. Kelly is nice…even if I have a sneaky feeling that I will not like what she has planned for this mannequin and me. "What is this about?" I ask, nodding my head towards the mannequin and promptly changing the subject.

"Therapy is all about an outlet…whether sadness, or anger, or whatever it is you are feeling. So, I thought I would mix it up a little today. Instead of just sitting and talking, I figured I would let you beat up this guy."

"Oh" is all I say.

"I also thought it would be good to have an outlet before your family session. Those can be a bit intense."

"It can be more intense than my last session with you? That is great," I say as I roll my eyes.

Kelly only smiles a calm smile. "Here." She hands me the bat.

I take it, albeit somewhat reluctantly.

"Katrina, I know you have been hurt, and I know you do not want to talk about it. I can see it…as someone who has been hurt…I can see it."

Suddenly, I understand why Kelly gets me so well and perhaps why I could not allow myself to not like her even though a part of me wanted to. She seems to be an understanding person, and I can only guess it is in a large part due to what she herself has been through. I do not say anything. I only nod my head slightly.

"I want you to picture the guy who hurt you as this mannequin. I want you to hit him with the bat, Katrina, and tell him he cannot hurt you anymore."

I lift the bat slowly and swing. "You cannot hurt me anymore." I say this with no emotion.

"Come on, Katrina, really hit him. He did this to you. You are here because of him."

I swing the bat harder now. "You cannot hurt me anymore!" I yell. I swing again, and again, and again. I swing until my arms are sore and tears soak my face. I scream until my throat is raw. I scream that he cannot hurt me anymore...until I almost believe it. When I finally relent, Kelly comes over. Gently, she takes the bat from my hand.

"You did real well today, Katrina. You should be proud of yourself."

But I do not feel proud. I just feel...drained, like I have nothing left to give.

CHAPTER THIRTY-TWO

I DEBATE ABOUT BAILING ON SCOTT. HOWEVER, HE WILL FIND ME eventually. Also, I really do want to see what it is he wants to show me. I also need a distraction more than ever now. I slip into the bathroom by the rec room and splash my face with cold water. I am glad that I had stopped bothering to wear makeup and make a mental note that if I am still here when I start to wear it again, I will not wear any on a day that I have therapy. Finally, after a few deep breaths, I gather my bearings and head outside to meet Scott.

It is now almost lunch time, and I wonder if he will be there waiting. *If he is not*, I say to myself, *I will retreat to my room*. I cannot stand to be in a room full of people right now. The sunshine feels good on my face, even though I can literally feel the summer slip into fall with each passing day. The sun almost blinds me, but I see him there just as clear as day. Scott sits on the bench, and as I get closer, I notice he has his notebook in his lap. It is the notebook I had seen him writing in that day in the rec room. I remember I had wanted to know what it was he wrote in there. Is that it? Is this my chance to really see into Scott? Even though he and I have become friends, we still have our walls up.

I sit next to Scott without saying a word.

"Do I dare ask how it went?" Scott asks.

Instead of answering his question, I say, "You are missing lunch. We can meet later if you like."

"If we meet later, you will probably not show, and I may chicken out of what I was going to show you. We would not want that now, would we?"

I smile a small smile. How this guy always knows how to make me smile without knowing me all that well is beyond me. I would almost go as far to say he even seems a little bit of a flirt today, a sense I never get from him. He never flirts with me or Jazzie. I am not sure if he is being careful not to, or if he does not even know how to flirt. I used to have to tell myself not to flirt because I was so natural at it. Now I just feel so sad all the time that it just does not come as easily as it used to.

"Okay," I say, finally turning to look at him. "What is it you want to show me? I have to admit, I have been curious," I confess.

Scott holds up his notebook in his hand. He grips it so tightly that it seems more like he is ready to guard it than show it to me. "I write, mainly poems. I write some short stories as well. My mother does not approve because she wants me to go into business, and I would never have the nerve to show the guys at school."

I sit quietly, not sure where Scott is going with this.

"I wrote a poem for my mom a while ago, though I still have not shared it with her. I am not sure I ever will." Scott pauses again, and I still feel unsure where this is going. "The poem sort of reminds me of you, though I do not know your story."

"I do not know yours," I point out.

"Would you like to know mine, Katrina?" Scott says, his voice dipping just a little lower than usual. He does not need to speak loudly, however, because we sit there alone. There are only two adults a few yards away, because of course they are always watching. However, all the kids are either at lunch or in their rooms.

"First, I would like to know what it is you wanted to show me. Then maybe you can tell me about your story?"

"Well, we shall see," Scott says, and, for a moment, his thoughts seem to be far away. Snapping back, Scott looks at me, those jade green eyes piercing right through me. "I would like for you to read the poem I wrote for my mom."

CHAPTER THIRTY-THREE

I HAVE NO IDEA WHAT READING A POEM ABOUT SCOTT'S MOTHER could have to do with me. However, I am certainly not going to say no.

"I would love to read the poem." I smile at Scott now. I can see him take a breath as he thumbs through his notebook to locate the poem. Moments later Scott hands me his notebook. "You do not want to read it to me?" I ask Scott.

"You are the only person who has ever seen what I have written, except for those I used for assignments in school. This is the first personal poem I have ever shared. I am nervous enough without reading it out loud," Scott admits and then goes on to say, "I just really think the poem...well, just read."

"Shattered" by Scott Eady

I see your pain
I know it is there
Though you try to be strong for me
You play like you do not care
You close off your heart
Because it is no longer there

Not as it used to be
It is shattered
You do not speak of the one
That did this to you
But I have heard the rumors
And the look in your sad eyes
Is all the proof
I know it is true
You only told your mum
She was sure to tell me
She meant to cause pain
Even though we are family
But she hurts too
Because someone damaged what is hers
Her daughter so pure
Robbed of a choice
And still she chose
To keep a reminder
Now I am the one who lives with this
But my pain is not my own
I weep for you mum
Together we feel alone
Together we are broken to the bone
Shattered.

I let the words sink in, dancing all around. Little pricks tingle all over my body, and my stomach feels like an empty pit. What does this mean? I think I know, yet I cannot find the words. I cannot handle this. I do not want to know any hurt that is in this guy's life because I do not want to think of him being hurt. I certainly do not want him to know about me, my dark secrets that I do not even whisper to myself.

I shove the notebook into Scott's lap hard and fast and am on my feet all in the same motion. I run back to the cabin and am halfway there before I hear Scott call to me, "Katrina, come back. Let me explain, please."

He says something else, but I do not hear it. I am up the steps and in my room in minutes. I do not bother to change out of my black stretch pants and gray T-shirt. The one highlight about not really caring what I wear and trying to impress anyone, it is the fact that I am always comfortable, or at least my clothes are. I sink down into my bed, even though it earns me demerits, and I miss my forth therapy session, because that is exactly where I stay for the next two days straight.

CHAPTER THIRTY-FOUR

By dinner time on that second night, I receive a visit from Kelly. I was expecting this. Of course, these people are to carry on trying to fix me. That is their job, after all. However, I do not expect what Kelly has to say. If I do not get out of this bed and eat an actual meal—"and more than three bites," Kelly informs me—I am going to be admitted to a hospital. There is a medical facility down the road, and I would be hooked up to an IV.

"Katrina, I think you would really benefit from the group therapy held on Thursday."

"But that group is for girls with eating disorders," I protest. "I eat just fine."

"When is the last time you ate?"

I sit quietly. I can't remember, and so I cannot answer Kelly. That is not a problem, though. I have always been a good eater, maybe not the healthiest, but I eat. Sure, maybe I have not been eating as much as I used to...not since...

"Listen." Kelly slices through my thoughts like a knife through butter, and I feel a sting in her next words. "Oftentimes when people go through a traumatic experience, they develop certain habits.

For example, not eating enough, self-harm and other various ways to deal with their pain."

"But I am not..." I protest loudly. Thankfully, my roommate is currently at dinner.

"I know you are not self-harming, Katrina, but not eating the way you are is harmful. I am sorry, and I know this is hard, but you are going to have to face what happened to you at some point so you can heal."

Suddenly I think of Scott's poem. "Shattered" was the title. "How do you heal something that is shattered," I asked. My voice was barely above a whisper.

"You heal by being here, Katrina. You heal by trying. By letting people help you get there."

"If I start eating, do I still have to go to that group therapy?" I ask. I can only take so much therapy in this place, and my family therapy is fast approaching. Of course, I only expect to see one person, my mom. I do have my mom and aunt. Maybe my aunt would come also. Still, it was enough to deal with.

"Okay. If you go to dinner right now and continue to eat each meal, then we can table the group therapy, at least for now." Kelly pauses, and then she looks right into my eyes to let me know she means her next words. "There are monitors in there, Katrina. I will know if you are really eating."

I nod my head silently. I slowly drag my body out of bed. My legs feel shaky to stand on. *Please, do not faint*, I silently say to myself. I do not faint. I drag a brush through my hair, and I make my way to the dining hall. On the way to the dining hall, my knees continue to feel weak and unsteady. However, it is not because the lack of food in my system. I am nervous to face Scott again, though I doubt he even wants to see me. I have not talked to Jazzie in two days either. I do not know if I can face either one of them, but if it had to be one or the other, I hope it will be Jazzie. She never gets serious on me, and she always makes me laugh. Suddenly, I find myself hoping to see her...but not Scott. I just could not face him yet.

All too soon I enter the dining hall. I see neither Scott nor Jazzie. I get my meal, thankfully just some plain cheese pizza. That is easy enough to start with. It takes me a half hour to get through the slice. I finish just as the last of the kids file out of the dining hall. I decide before I head back that I will try my luck and see if I can go visit Jazzie. Special permission is needed to be able to go to other cabins. So many rules—I am not even sure how I keep them straight.

At first, the woman, Maxine, who was a regular monitor in the dining hall, did not even remember who I was talking about. "Oh, right, Jasmine Grey. I suppose only her friends call her Jazzie. Yes, I remember now. You sat with her and that other boy, Scott. Yes, he was here earlier, poor guy, sitting by himself..."

I listen as she prattles on. Wait...

"Excuse me, but I am really just looking for Jazzie...um, Jasmine. Would it be okay to visit her, just for a few minutes?"

"Oh, honey, she left yesterday."

"What?!"

CHAPTER THIRTY-FIVE

As I make my way back to my cabin, I feel more defeated than ever. It is like I am constantly taking one step forward and three steps back, punched and kicked down on a constant basis. I stop at the bench where Scott and I always sat, missing my friend. I have no one. I have only made two friends after being here for two weeks, and I have managed to push one away, and now the other has left without so much as a goodbye. I know I just dipped out on Jazzie with no contact for a few days now. Would Scott not have told Jazzie what happened? Perhaps she was not able to contact me. Did something happen to Jazzie? Had I just missed the signs because I am so damn wrapped up in my own drama? I know for a fact she did not tell me she was leaving anytime soon. But we never talked about any of that stuff. I do not even know why she was here or what she had been through. Can I even call myself her friend? *Some friend I am*, I think to myself. A real friend would be concerned, would have asked more about what she had been through. What do I even know about this girl?

"I am such a shitty friend." I bend my head down and cover my face with both hands as tears threaten my eyes. I squeeze them closed tightly.

"I would not say you were a shitty friend. You have just been through a lot of shit."

I do not need to pry my eyes open to know who said that. Scott's voice covers me like a warm blanket, and yet it gives me chills all at the same time. Suddenly, I open my eyes. I need to start facing things...and people. Scott stands in front of me only two feet away, hesitation clear on his face, his shoulders tensed and body rigid.

"I do not think I have ever heard you curse before."

One tear escapes my eye, but a small smile creeps its way over my lips as I look up at Scott. I stand up, and I see the sadness take over Scott's face. He must think I am going to take off again. But I smile up at him.

"Follow me," I say this, my voice soft.

Scott nods his head and gestures with his hand, indicating me to lead the way. I do just that, and Scott follows. Even though I do not watch him follow, I can feel the heat of his body as he keeps close to me. The scent of him dances in the air around me, and I try to ignore it. I need a clear head for what is to come next.

CHAPTER THIRTY-SIX

I WALK OVER TO THE SMOKING SECTION. YEAH, I KNOW ONE STEP forward and three steps back. I just need a cigarette to calm my nerves, because I know I am about to have an important conversation. I am not starting to smoke again—I just need one. Perhaps it does not make sense. Not much makes sense to me these days. I do know I need to start facing things in my life though, and I decide I will start with repairing my friendships. I will write that letter to Alyssa later. But right now, Scott is here in the flesh, and we have so much to talk about.

Thankfully, there is only one person in the smoking section. It generally gets busy right after dinner and then dies down for the rest of the night. Also, thankfully, that one person has a spare cigarette. I think her name is Julie. She is in my cabin, so I have seen her around. I thank her, and she even returns my smile, so I decide she is good people. However, I cannot wait for her to leave so I can start this conversation, because if I do not leap into what I have to say, I just might chicken out. She does not take too long to leave, and I decide to start with an easy question for Scott. "Have you talked to Jazzie? I heard she left."

"No, actually, that day...you know..."

"That day I was a jerk of a friend and ran away?"

Scott smiles at my words. "Well, glad to know that we are still friends. Anyway, that day she was not in the dining hall, and I had not heard anything. I did not realize she left."

"Yeah, that is what the lady in the dining hall said...Maxine...she said she left."

"Hmm. That is too bad. She seemed to be a good person... and funny too. Well, bad for us, but most likely good for her, anyway."

"Yeah," I smile, but my smile quickly falls. "Scott...your poem...it was a great poem. But if that was about your mom, I have to ask, was she raped?"

Scott sucks his breath in and lowers his head, his light brown hair falling over his eyes. "Yes, and I was the result. My grandmother told me one day. I do not think she meant to. It just kind of came out. Kind of messes with your head, knowing your dad is a rapist." Scott looks up at me now.

I look at him reassuringly. "You can tell me Scott, but only if you want to," I say.

He does not lower his head as he continues, "the story I was told was that she was attacked one night after work. She had been with boys before, or at least that is what she told me. My grandmother believed she had not even been with a boy in that way at all. I do not even know if she is telling me the truth that she does not know who it is. My mother likes to keep things in from people...she is not as hard as everyone believes her to be. I see the pain she is in when she thinks I am not looking. The woman does know how to dig her heels in, however. I am sure she will never tell anyone if she knew her attacker or not."

"Oh, Scott, I am so sorry. You know you are not him, though. Is this why you do not date?"

"I guess it is part of it. I also do want to get my life together before I devote myself to someone. So, what about you? What happened to you, Katrina?" Scott changes the subject to me...and this is the part I am most afraid of.

CHAPTER THIRTY-SEVEN

"THAT WAS FAST," I SAY, MAYBE A BIT TOO HARSHLY BECAUSE SCOTT physically backs away from me.

"Sorry, I...I am just concerned about you, Katrina."

"Why?" I ask, and I really want to know.

"I do not know," Scott answers right away. "I cannot really describe why, honestly...I just feel this pull toward you." He pauses, and his brows pull together, as if he is being careful with his words, or trying to be, anyway. "I feel like I was literally born to protect you. I know that sounds absolutely crazy but..." He drops his head as if not wanting to face my reaction.

"Well, we are in the right place for that, I suppose," I say, trying to lighten this moment that I know we both feel the weight of. Scott does not laugh at what I say. He does not even look up. I continue to explain to him how I felt. "Look, full confession. I felt a pull toward you when I saw you too. I felt...like I wanted to help you, but like I was scared at the same time. It did not make sense to me either," I admit to him, and this is the most truth I have spoken since I graduated, since the night my world got turned upside down.

"Maybe..." Scott hesitates. "Maybe we are supposed to help each other."

"Maybe we are," I agree.

"You can talk to me, Katrina. I would never judge you."

"Listen, I am not ready to get into detail. It is just too hard. I will say this. I was not raped...but I was assaulted. I am trying to find my voice and get through this. Which finding my voice apparently does not mean burning down a shed in the woods...where it happened... and what landed me here."

"Ah." This is all Scott says. Then he continues, "I am sorry that happened to you, Katrina. I am going to state the obvious now and say it was not your fault. Also, thank you. Thank you for confiding in me."

"It is the most I have ever spoken about it, and that includes even to myself when I am all alone."

"Well, then, I feel honored that you feel comfortable enough with me to share this much of yourself. I should have known you did something bold."

"Bold?" I laugh. "I am not bold. That would be my friend Alyssa."

"Well, I would love to meet this friend," Scott says and smiles.

With that, I grow quiet. *If Alyssa will still be my friend*, I think silently. Then I realize something. "Hey..." I say to Scott. "You told me about your mom. You never said why you are here, though."

"Oh, right," Scott says, and he grows solemn and serious. He stays quiet for a minute, and I try to remain calm and patient for him to speak again. Every passing second, I swear that the beat of my heart grows louder and louder, and my skin begins to itch with anticipation. When I feel as if I cannot take it anymore, Scott begins to speak again. "I had learned the truth about my mom, and well, my existence. Then, I do not know, school and everything, it just all did not seem to matter. It was stressful, but it seemed all meaningless at the same time. I just could not take it anymore, so I tried to end it."

Now my eyes brim with hot tears. "How," I ask. Part of me wants to take it back as soon as it has escaped my lips, but another part, a bigger part, wants to know. Because even with all that I had been through, I just never thought of that as an option. I am far from healthy, and I know not eating could have the potential to hurt me. I just could never end it in one instant like that. I felt I was too much of a coward. But is taking your own life a kind of cowardly thing to do in itself, to give up on life like that? Now my heart aches for the Scott, who felt that was his only option. It is a physically painful ache.

Scott does not answer me in words. He holds up his left hand, and my own hand instantly goes to the inch-long scar that lie longways down his forearm by his wrist. Why have I never noticed that before?

"I actually passed out before I got to the other arm. They said it probably saved my life. Basically, I am such a failure I could not even do this right."

"What!" Suddenly, I am mad at Scott. "Do not ever say that! Do you hear me? Scott, you are so brave. I am so glad I met you."

Then Scott does something that shocks the shit out of me. He kisses me.

CHAPTER THIRTY-EIGHT

When Scott brings his lips to mine, my body instantly reacts as if I have lost total control over my actions. My head feels dizzy and my mind in a fog. I feel warmth spread throughout my entire body, and I kiss him back hard. My body melts into his like hot lava. Then just as quickly, Scott pulls away.

"Sorry. Katrina, I am so sorry...I..." Scott hangs his head. He looks full of regret. I cannot stand to be with him for another minute. It is clear he regrets kissing me. I bolt back to the cabin, straight to my room and my bed.

The next morning, I do not stay in my bed and sulk. I decide to write my letter to Alyssa.

> Alyssa,
>
> I am so sorry I have not spoken to you. I have just not had the nerve. I could not stand to tell you why I burned that shed down. I just hurt so much. I will not say who caused the pain and I will not say why. I just cannot. Not yet anyway. I will say that I forgive you for telling on me. I know you were just concerned for me. I am not even sorry that I have landed here at this

> place. I think it is helping...or it will be the thing to break me. I feel it could go one way or the other from one minute to the next. I hope I make it through, and I hope we can still be friends. Best friends for life. I miss you. I wish I could say more. But I will get there, and I hope you will still be there when I do.
>
> ~Katrina

After I write the letter to Alyssa, I feel a slight weight lift off my shoulders. Perhaps I should mail the letter to her. I do miss her. I tear it out of my notebook and put it on my dresser by the box of envelopes that my mother insisted I bring. I know she expects a letter from me. Family therapy is coming up in a couple of days. I will see her then, so I put off writing her a letter. However, maybe I could write one to Scott. Not to give to him, but I need to sort out these feelings I am having. I felt better after writing my letter to Alyssa—why not a letter to Scott?

I decide I need to get out of my room to write him. I just hope I do not run into him in the process. I am not avoiding him exactly. I just need to gather my thoughts. This letter may be just the thing that could help with that. I decide to head to the rec room. I slowly make my way to the rec room, keeping an eye out for Scott. As I tentatively approach the rec room, I am relieved to see only two girls who seemed to be occupied, one of which is the friendly girl who had given me a cigarette the night before. The other I do not recognize. I smile at the girl I recognize, who glances up briefly, and I take a seat in the corner of the couch.

I stare at the blank paper for what feels like hours. I look at the clock. Fifteen whole minutes have gone by, not hours. I grit my teeth, suck in my breath, and then release the breath as I put pen to paper.

Scott,

I am at a loss for words.

This is true. I am at a loss for words. *Okay*, I tell myself, *clear your mind and speak from how you feel*. But how the hell do I feel? I had been on dates with guys in the past. Well, hung out with a few anyway, not one of them had ever confused me in this way. Also, not one of them had I ever cared about or felt they cared about me, not really. Why do I feel as if I care about this guy? This is a guy, who has pushed me away not once, but twice now. Sure, the second time he kissed me first, but it was clear to me that he regretted it. Perhaps I have pushed him away too and so that is not a fair assessment. However, I have never had the experience of the guy resisting, it has always been me. This guy is different though, clearly. This is a guy, who does not seem to "want only one thing." A guy who shared some shocking things about his past, and he did not once judge when I shared my own demons of the past. The guy with the hat that shaded his jade green eyes on that first day we met. Eyes that seemed to see right to my very soul before either of us had spoken a word to each other and every day after that. What is it about Scott Eady that has my thoughts spinning? What is it about him that makes me feel this way? It cannot be just that he is different than other guys I have come across in the past. There must be more to it than that. Or perhaps I am completely overthinking the entire thing. However, if it was so simple then why can I not put my feelings into words and make sense of it all?

CHAPTER THIRTY-NINE

As the minutes tick by, I continue to be at a loss for words. I never realized how hard feelings are to put into actual words when it comes to the heart. Then panic sets in. What if I write the letter and somehow, he sees it? I finally give up and make my way up to my room. My family session is in two days. I decide to wait to mail Alyssa's letter until after that and for now put off writing one to Scott. I have too many thoughts swirling around in this head of mine. The aching feeling in the pit of my stomach will not subside until after my family session. Then, maybe some of my thoughts will make a little more sense.

Still, I feel a sort of sense of defeat as I make my way to my room. As I enter my room, Nia lies on her bed, reading a book as usual. "Want to join me for a smoke?"

I look around to see if anyone else has entered my room. Surely, I had hallucinated, and Nia was not asking me to join her outside.

"Me?" I ask.

Nia rolls her eyes. That is more like it. "Yes you."

"But don't you hate me?" I guess honesty is my new thing. I think this place is doing something to me where I say whatever is on my mind. This is not like me at all. Usually, I care most about sparing people's feelings. But not speaking up got me here in the first place, hadn't it? Perhaps this new way is better. Besides, it is easier here. After I leave here, I will never see these people again, right?

"You need to lighten up, girl." Nia says this like it is just a simple fact she is stating. "I mean—" she smiles now—"I did not particularly like you, but you seem okay, I guess."

It is my turn to roll my eyes, and I laugh. Maybe this girl is not so bad after all. "All right, let's go."

We head outside in silence. Once outside I decide to take advantage of my newfound mindset to say whatever was on my mind and ask Nia a question I had been dying to ask since my first day. "So, what's up with all the psycho books?"

Nia laughs. "Why do you ask? Scared I am going to chop you into little pieces in your sleep?"

"Yeah maybe I am, kind of."

A roar of laughter ensues from Nia to the point she is doubled over in laughter and can barely catch a breath. Finally, Nia says, "you know I am just a 17-year-old girl like you, right?"

"Hey, killers come in all shapes, sizes, and ages. You should know that by reading all those books of yours."

"I want to be a psych major, Katrina. That is, if I ever make it out of this place. My teacher, well former teacher, suggested I read these books while in here. She thought it could be a way to look into how the mind works."

"Your teacher never thought how that may look to a potential roommate?"

"No, I guess she did not," Nia smiles. "Tell me, what do you want to do when you get out of here?"

It is my turn to be taken aback. I have never even asked myself that question. I decide to go with honesty once again. "Live. Other than that, I have no idea." I stare out into space for a moment, thinking. "Maybe write. I do not know, not sure if I would even be any good at it. I used to write short stories, but that seems like a long time ago. I also wanted to work with children once upon a time, but I just do not feel that is for me now. Writing seems like more of a possibility, but, honestly, I have no idea."

"Ah, probably just feels that way," Nia says, waving her cigarette. I had passed on having one. I really need to kick the habit, and besides, it is not the same without the burn of alcohol to follow. "I think time just kind of goes slower here. Most likely due to the fact we think about things so much here. It just gets too heavy a lot of the time."

"Nia," I ask.

"Yeah," Nia responds.

"How long have you been here?"

"Five very long months," she sighs.

I grow quiet. Could I survive five long months of this? Nia seems to read my thoughts. "But hey," she says, "everyone is different."

"I have my family therapy day after tomorrow."

"Oh, man. Well, good luck. Mine was tough. But my parents being divorced, it is not like they can get along. I was surprised my dad showed up. I am also sure they do not even remember what it is like to be a teenager, either one of them. Your mom seems more chill."

"Yeah, I guess."

"Well, I will tell you what. I will distract you tomorrow so you will not think about it too much."

I smile at Nia. "Be careful Nia. I may think that we are friends." With that, we both burst into a fit of laughter.

CHAPTER FORTY

NIA AND I ARE SEPARATED FOR A GOOD PART OF THE DAY, AS EVERY-one has different schedules of chores. When lunchtime comes around, we decide to skip it and hang out in the rec room instead. I know Kelly will be monitoring if I go to my meals, but I make a mental note to speak with her later and explain. Hopefully if I do explain to Kelly before she has the chance to approach me this will be enough that I will not have to face any consequences by not going to lunch today. Besides, each building has a vending machine, so Nia grabs some Doritos, and I grab some vanilla cookies—voilà. Lunch is served. I know Doritos are a teenage staple, but I could just never get into them.

"You are crazy, girl. These things are awesome, almost up there with pizza and a cold beer." This is Nia's response when I share my distaste of the cheesy chips.

"They just do not do it for me," I say, shrugging my shoulders. "I will agree with the pizza and beer, though." I smile.

"Hey, you know," Nia says, "you really are all right."

I smile at her. I am beginning to think she is all right too. Then I think of something else I have wanted to know about but never had the nerve to ask. "Hey, Nia, if you don't mind me asking, what was the deal with you and Jazzie?"

"Simple," Nia stated. "She slept with the only boy I ever loved while we were together, and she was supposed to be my friend once-upon-a-time. Honestly though, we grew apart years before that. Still does not excuse her from sleeping with Jake that is his name."

"Oh."

"I think she was somehow trying to make up for what she did to me by helping you to get with Scott. But the damage between us is already done. I mean, I am past it. This was last year, but I could never be friends with her again."

Everything makes a lot more sense now. Slightly cautious about adding fuel to fire, I have to ask one more question. "Any idea what happened to her, anyway? She just disappeared."

"She did not disappear, Katrina. She just went home. We got here at the same time. One night when we were out partying, I confronted her...a huge fight ensued, things escalated, and poof, we both end up here."

"Oh, wow," I respond, not really knowing what else to say. "But wait...how come you are still here?"

"Her parents probably yanked her out. She has money, I do not. Plain, and simple as that." Nia says this all very plainly and to the point. I guess Nia sees I need more because she continues. "Listen, I am not saying she was the worst person in the world, but Jazzie can turn on people for no reason. It is not even really her fault. It is just kind of how her parents are and so she is too. If she wants something, she does not seem to care who gets in the way. Like I said, she learned this from her parents. But who knows? Maybe she will change."

I think about this. The more I found out about people it seems the less I know, and I do not know who to trust. "How long were you friends?" Maybe that will shed some perspective on how much of

Nia's word I should believe when it comes to Jazzie. She was my first friend here, after all, when I needed one the most.

"Since kindergarten...but we grew apart as soon as we got into high school. We just became very different people. We both started hanging out in different crowds. Then she slept with Jake, and I just could not forgive her after that. I mean, I am past it, but I cannot forgive her as in be friends with her ever again." Nia pauses as if questioning what to say next or lost in her own thoughts. "You know, I was not sure what to make of you when you first arrived, then you became friends with her, and I did not like you. But I could see after a while that you are different. You are okay, Katrina."

"Well, I'll toast to that." I smile and hold up a cookie.

Nia promptly holds up a chip, and we clang them together. We smile at each other, and for the first time, I notice Nia has dimples. She does not look so scary after all. But then she asks a question that I hate to even think about.

"I have to ask, why do you hate being called Kat? I feel like your name is so long."

"That is because your name is three letters," I answer.

"And you are completely evasive," Nia replies.

"A guy used to call me that...a guy I do not want to talk about." I feel my cheeks flush. Nia must catch on that this is a sore subject because she changes the topic immediately.

"So, what is up with you and Mr. Green Eyes anyway?" Nia smiles and raises her eyebrows up and down.

"Oh, my goodness, that is what I called him before I knew his name!" I spit. Nia and I grow into a fit of laughter only fit for teenage girls.

As we sat letting the laughter die down, if only for a moment, Nia says, "But seriously, what is up? I saw you guys hanging out."

"Yeah, we are just friends," I say. "He does not date. How about that you and that Carl guy?"

Nia blushes and then goes on to tell me all about Carl, only about half of which I hear as my thoughts drift back and forth to Scott.

CHAPTER FORTY-ONE

The topic of Carl dwindles down, and Nia and I talk about basic things for the rest of the night—movies, music, books, and even family. I learn Nia lives with her mom just as I live with mine, only she does know her dad. However, she reveals she sees him less and less these days. Her mom is "okay," as Nia puts it, but "does not really get her or being a teenager at all." Even though Nia's appearance is sort of punk meets emo, Nia is into a variety of music and movies just like I am. She is also into other books, but her recent passion has been the way the human mind works. She even says being here has made her want to be a therapist even more than before, though she admits she still has a slight problem with authority.

"Yeah, I totally get that. I mean, I am mostly a good kid, but I have a problem with people telling me what to do sometimes. I can have a bit of a temper at times."

"I cannot picture that," Nia says and smiles. We are now back in the room, and it is almost time to turn the light out.

"I think it is because I am a Gemini," I say. "On the one hand, I can be super sweet, and then something will set me off and my temper takes over. I swear, sometimes it is like my attitude has a mind of its own. It is my own evil twin."

The room has become silent. I look over at Nia and she is fast asleep. I smile to myself. She really is okay. But now that she is asleep, I am left to my own thoughts. I wonder if my aunt will come tomorrow. I wonder what Scott is doing. I wonder why I did not see him today. Soon, the darkness takes over, and I drift off to sleep.

"No!" I shout, my body thrashing about. "I said don't touch me!" In the darkness I feel his hands slipping down my panties, touching me where no one ever should without permission. He hooks his fingers and tears my panties off in one motion, not being gentle about it at all. His nails graze and sting my skin as he does. His breath is hot and smells of beer. It reminds me of soured milk, and I want to vomit. His heavy body is pressed up against mine in the small shack.

"Kitty Kat, come on," he says. "Let me taste your kitty-cat. I just want a little taste. You know you want me to."

I say no again, but I can feel his fingers slide in me. Two of his fingers are inside of me, and he is being so rough, his nails scratching my tender skin. His dirty fingers have invaded me. I feel paralyzed. Just as I feel as if I will die right there, he removes his fingers. "Don't fucking move." He slurs this, sweat beading his forehead.

Then he starts to take off his pants. This is not happening, not here, not now, and not like this. He is now exposed. Now is my chance. I muster all the energy I have, though the alcohol I have consumed has slowed my movements. I kick him as hard as I can. It gets the job done.

"You bitch! You are a fucking tease! You bitch!" he yells, grabbing himself, and I run. I leave my panties behind that he tore off me.

Thankfully my skirt is still on, so I am not completely naked from the waist down. The shack is not too far from my house, and I run all the way there. I am sweating and panting as I reach my house. Tears have stained my face and blurred my vision. And then I feel a hand on my arm.

Wait. I am home, safe. Who is touching me? I open my eyes.

I am not home. I am back at Stone Gates, and even in the darkness I can see the concern on Nia's face. "Do you want to talk about it?"

"He always invades my dreams. I wish he would go away already. I cannot even speak his name…what he did…" The tears are flowing down my face, soaking my cheeks.

Nia tentatively sits beside me on the bed. "You were raped, weren't you?"

"He tried. I can still feel his hands on me every time I close my eyes."

"You fought back?" Nia asks.

"I kicked him…hard. Then I ran. A few weeks later I burned down the shed where it happened. When my mom found out I was the one that burned it down she brought me here. I was never able to tell her why I did it. She must think I am crazy. I feel as if I am these days."

"You are not crazy Katrina. You are here to get help. You know, Kelly was assaulted. She is a good person to talk to. I have been seeing her for five months, and she's really been helping me." Nia grows quiet. "I have not been completely honest with you."

My expression starts to change to anger. I just bared my soul, and this girl has not even been honest with me? Nia continues to talk. "I have not lied. I just did not share the whole story. After the fight with Jasmine, we were both arrested. My parents left me in there overnight to 'teach me a lesson.' I was so pissed I went out the next night and got really drunk. I mean, I could not even walk. This guy offered me a ride. I barely remember having sex with him. To be honest, I do not even remember if I said no."

My mouth hangs open. I do not know what to say.

Nia goes on, "it messed me up, though. My parents knew something was wrong, even though they did not know about what happened. They assumed it was because of my break-up with Jake. But Katrina...I tried to take my own life. I will not get into that in detail, but the next day, I came here, and I found out Jazzie had come here as well soon after I arrived. She had gotten here a couple of weeks before me. I am assuming the last straw was our fight for her parents. Though I heard around school she had been getting into trouble, not sure of the details. Like I told you before, we had grown apart, and we did not speak unless it was to insult each other the whole time here.

Nia's confession makes my head spin as I lay back down to sleep. Maybe I am not so alone in this battle I have been having within myself after all. Perhaps there were others out there, others who could understand and not judge me because of what has happened to me. I lay there wondering this as I fell back into slumber. I also wondered about Jazzie, if I would ever know her story and what she had been through or if I would ever see her again.

CHAPTER FORTY-TWO

THE NEXT DAY I WAKE WITH BLURRED MEMORIES OF MY DREAM AND Nia's confession. Though her experience was a bit different than mine, I somehow feel not so alone anymore. It had even been confirmed for me that Kelly was assaulted as well, though if I am being honest, I knew this when she had told me in therapy that she was someone who has been hurt. Deep down, I had known what she meant without saying the actual words.

My mind then drifts to Scott. I have not seen or talked to him in two days. Things feel so unresolved in every aspect of my life right now. In just a few short hours after lunch today, I will have my group therapy. My first one ever, and to say I am nervous is a tremendous understatement.

I decide to go for a walk to clear my head. As I walk around, I spot Scott. He sits at our bench, writing, his head lowered as his hair falls slightly in his face. I swallow down the lump that is beginning to form in my throat and walk over. "Hey."

Scott looks up from his writing. "Hello, Katrina." He says this in a low tone. He looks nervous, perhaps afraid his words may send me off running once again. Little does he know; however, I feel about as nervous as he looks. I overcome my nerves and sit down next to Scott with determination. I cannot lose his friendship. He has become too important in the short time that I have known him. Everything between us is all so unresolved, and I will not give up without a fight, or at least some answers.

"Why don't you like me?" I blurt out what is in my heart before my head has a chance to stop it. "What I mean to say is why are you not interested in me the way that I am into you?" I have no idea where I am getting the nerve to ask such a thing. Before coming here, before meeting Scott, I would have not even cared about such a thing. But it nags at me, and I need answers. I cannot ask my father why he never knew me. I cannot ask Grant why he would hurt me the way he did. Scott, however, sits before me, and I can ask him. So, I seize the moment. At this point, what do I really have to lose?

"Fancy a walk?" Scott asks. I hesitate. "Come on, then. I have found a new place I want to show you."

How can I resist? I get up and follow Scott. He leads me to the building next to ours and around the side. As we round the corner, the fresh scent of laundry hits my nose. Scott leads me in the doorway, where, sure enough, five washers and five dryers line the wall. A couple of the washers spin around, filling the room with a lovely scent. The scent reminds me of home, making my heart ache to be there again.

Scott walks past the washers and dryers to another door. This door goes to another room. Inside there is a couch and a table with a dusty magazine on top. "Is this where you have been? The reason I have not seen you for two days?"

"You have not seen me because I have been a coward, Katrina, too scared to face you. But, yes, this is where I have been. It is a good thinking spot, actually."

"Are you scared of me?" I sit on the couch, and Scott does the same.

"You are so strong, Katrina. I have never met anyone like you. You go for what you want. You are not a coward like me. So, yes, I find it a little scary. But it is so much more than that. I am afraid of these feelings I am having for you. It is unlike anything I have felt before."

I sit listening to Scott in shock.

"Katrina, I have not been able to stop thinking about you since you walked into that building the first day. I spotted you as soon as you walked in, wishing I could disappear, embarrassed by my mom. Then, when you looked into my eyes' that was it, I knew I wanted to get to know you."

"To get to know me to be friends," I ask, hesitantly taking my eyes off my own hands folded in my lap where they had been to meet his brilliant green eyes.

"I do not think friends feel this way," Scott says as he reaches out a hand to caress my cheek. Automatically, my eyes close and I let my face mold into his hand.

"Then why did you deny me?"

"I told you. I am a coward. When I really thought about it, I realized what I am most scared of. Thinking about it these past two days has taught me that."

"What is that?" I ask, my own eyes never leaving Scott's.

"I am most scared of the way I feel when I am not around you. Katrina, I do not want to be apart from you. I do not think I can bear it. It is so scary for me to think of being with someone. I ran from it my whole life, avoided it at all costs. However, to think of being apart from you, Katrina, it quite literally makes me feel as though I cannot breathe at the mere thought."

At these words I push my hands into Scott's hair, bringing his lips to mine. His confession is so raw and pure that it sparks something deep inside me. Something that I never knew could exist, least of all for me. A fire has ignited in me, burning from deep inside. Flames dance upon my skin, burning and sparking all around me. This time, Scott does not pull away.

CHAPTER FORTY-THREE

Scott's tongue caresses mine, and I feel my body quite literally melt. His hands are on my waist, and mine are tangled in his hair. Then suddenly, panic takes over, and I am the one to pull away.

"Wait," I pant, short of the breath he has stolen from me. "What does this mean? I mean, what will we do when we leave here? You live only an hour away, and I live three and a half hours away."

"I thought you wanted this...wanted me."

I can see doubt has crept its way into those green eyes. I need to be gentle with him, I know that. While I have distanced myself mentally from guys, I have had experience. Scott has had none. If I am being honest, I have kissed a lot of boys. But if I dive deeper into honesty, no one has ever made me feel this way. Now that I know Scott feels the same, there is no denying that. And there is no going back. But we do need to be realistic.

I take a breath as I choose my next words with caution. "I do, Scott. You are the first guy I have really wanted. I cannot even explain it, really. I was drawn to you, just as you were drawn to me from that first day. That is why I want to talk to you and know what it is we both intend. I do not ever want to hurt you, and truth be told...I do not think I could be apart from you either. Not now, especially now that I know you feel the same. But look around." I smile gently to try and ease the truth. "We are in a place because we both have issues, and we live miles away."

"Look, I know it will not be easy. But life has not been easy for us thus far, right?'

"True." I have to agree with him there.

"Plus," he points out, "who else could ever understand our issues more than each other?"

I could not deny how much truth was in that. In a way, we are both victims of sexual assault. I had been violated, and he was a product of rape.

"A fine pair we make," Scott states.

I laugh at this and then soften my smile as I look at Scott. He is breathtaking. "How have you never had a girlfriend before?"

Scott blushes. "I never wanted one before."

"Is that what I am?"

"You are if you want to be."

"For the first time ever, I do. I want to be someone's girlfriend. I never wanted that title before." I stare off in thought for a moment.

"What is wrong?" Scott asks, furrowing his brows together in concern.

"I do not think we should tell anyone, at least not our moms and at least not until we are out of here."

Scott considers this. "I hate to say it, but I think you may be right about that."

"Your mom is not going to like that you met your first girlfriend in here." I half smile and half cringe at this thought.

"You let me deal with my mom."

"You never answered my question," I probe once again.

"Oh, and what question was that?"

"What will happen when we leave here? We live so far away from each other, Scott."

"Well, I was actually going to give college a try. Were you?"

"I suppose I want to. I think I want to be a writer." I had been toying with the idea for a while now, but it all seemed like an impossible dream. This is the effect Scott has on me—he makes me want to dream.

"What a coincidence. I have just decided to shove business school and pursue writing." Scott grins from ear to ear. "Perhaps we can go to the same college."

"Oh boy, that and dating me—your mom is not going to be happy. Oh no," I begin to panic. "What if she thinks I pushed you into writing and blames me? Oh boy, she is going to hate me."

"Hey." Scott rubs my arm gently. "I told you I will deal with my mom. Besides, she already knows writing is a passion of mine. I have just never had the courage to pursue it before, until now."

"I just...I do not know. I want her to like me. She is a big part of you, you know."

"Do not worry, darling. Today you only need worry about your mom. You have your family therapy today, yes?"

"Oh yeah I do." That aching feeling in my stomach returns at the thought. "I cannot believe you remembered that."

Scott smiles his bright smile. "I pay attention. You know when it comes to my girlfriend."

Now I am the one smiling from ear to ear. My smile fades as I hear a noise from the other side of the door. Scott heard it the same time I did, and we both grow quiet. If we get caught in here, we will be in so much trouble. Soon, the noise disappears, and in unison we release a breath we had both been holding in.

"Maybe we should head back to the bench," Scott suggests.

"Wait," I grab Scott's arm as he goes to stand up from the couch. "Let's wait to make sure the coast is clear."

Scott nods, and I lean into him, my soft lips caressing his. I think that I like having a boyfriend.

CHAPTER FORTY-FOUR

As the hours turn to minutes before my family therapy session, I grow more and more nervous with anticipation. Scott and I sit on the bench and talk for a few minutes. However, I want to go to my room to collect my thoughts and gather my nerve before the therapy session. At a quarter to two, I hear familiar voices out in the hall. Is that...

I open the door to my room to be greeted by both my mother and Alyssa. At the sight of Alyssa, tears come to my eyes. It has been so long. I need my best friend back.

"Please, tell me that means that you are not mad I am here. I just missed you so much, and then I ran into your mom last week, and she told me about your therapy session this week. She...I don't know...thought maybe it would be good if I came," Alyssa rattles on as if speaking one long sentence. "Hey, aren't the tears supposed to be saved for the actual therapy session?" Now Alyssa's eyes are misted with tears as well. We throw our arms around each other.

"Oh, Lys, I missed you so much. I even wrote you a note." I go over to my dresser. The note sits on top right where I left it. "Well, here." I hand Alyssa the note, though I suppose it does not matter much now. I am sure we will do plenty of talking in therapy. I just hope not too much. I do not think I am ready for all to be revealed just yet. I can feel myself getting stronger. I am close. *I just need a little more time*, I tell myself.

I give my mother, who knows how important Alyssa is and has been waiting patiently, a huge hug as Alyssa unfolds the note and reads it. My mother squeezes me back tightly, understanding that I am not only saying hello, but also thanking her for bringing Alyssa here with her today. After Alyssa has finished reading the note, she looks at me with sympathetic eyes. "I am so sorry that I told on you about what you did to the shed. I was just so worried about you, and you were not talking to me. You really do look so much better…happier…than you were. I think this place could be working for you."

Yeah, that and the fact that I spent a good part of my day making out with the most gorgeous guy I have ever laid eyes on. He asking me to be his girlfriend did not hurt my current "happier" state of mind either. How I wish I could share the news with my best friend, but I just cannot, not while I am still in here.

"So, I have a little bit of gossip before we head into your session."

My mind, lost in thought, does not even register what Alyssa is saying. "What?" I ask, slightly dazed in memories of Scott's tongue molding into mine, his hands soft yet strong as they held my body to his.

"I said I have news. It is not even just gossip because it is a fact. It is kind of shocking, though."

I look straight at Alyssa now, giving her my full attention. A little gossip may be just the ticket to ease my nerves about the therapy session about to take place.

"Well, you know that new guy? Grant Jessup?"

I swear my heart literally stops beating at the mention of his name. Oh my god…did he try to assault someone else? I stand there frozen, voices around me fading away.

"Katrina, are you okay? You look pale suddenly. Did you hear about it already? I am so sorry, am I upsetting you? I did not even think that you liked the guy." Alyssa prattles on again.

Somehow, I cannot find my voice to tell her I have not heard any news. To tell her that the mere mention of his name makes my stomach ill and makes me want to crawl in a hole and bury myself there. Finally, I manage to shake my head no.

"You did not hear the news, then?" Alyssa asks.

"No," I manage to say in a small whimper.

"He died," Alyssa says.

What? Did I just hear her correctly, or have I truly gone mad?

"What?" I ask so low that it is barely a whisper.

"Yeah," Alyssa states. "Last week Grant was in a car accident on Hillside Avenue that road with all the sharp turns that goes up the mountain side?" Alyssa asks this but does not wait for my response as she continues to tell me what happened. "Well, it had rained the night before and Grant was drinking. He literally drove right off the side of the mountain into the water. It happened the day after I ran into your mom. That is crazy, right?"

Crazy...yes, I suppose I am going crazy. Wait... I guess that was not an actual question for me to answer. What is happening right now? My chest feels like it cannot catch breath. It feels heavy as if someone much stronger than me is pressing on it with all their strength. A drumming in my ear makes it impossible to hear all the words floating around. Grant Jessup...is dead?

"It is true," says Alyssa, as if confirming the thoughts, I had not spoken out loud. "Grant Jessup is dead."

"Why the hell, are you talking about my cousin?" a voice comes from the corner. It is Nia. What did she just say?

I turn around to face the doorway. Nia stands there with her hands on her hips. My mouth grows dry, and it feels as if my entire throat is depriving me of air, swollen from the dry lump that now sits there. "You...you're...you're what? Gra...what?" I cannot even form words.

"Yes, Grant is my cousin. How do you know him?" Nia looks at me now. She really looks at me, taking in my eyes that have grown wide with tears and the paleness that has taken over my face. "Wait..." Nia's face twists in realization. I am not sure how, but somehow Nia does not need to hear me say it to realize what that name means to me. "Oh Katrina, he is the guy you told me about, isn't he?"

"What guy?" My mother asks this, looking at me with suspicion. Alyssa just stands there silent, looking a bit confused. Nia looks at both, my mother and Alyssa, as if noticing them standing there for the first time, and then she looks back at me. I look at Nia now and all it takes is a slight nod of my head for Nia to know that it is true. Grant, who is apparently her cousin, is the one that assaulted me. She quickly turns and bolts down the hallway.

I hear someone say, "Whoa, slow down Nia." It is Kelly and she comes to stand in the doorway. "Katrina, are you ready for your group therapy session?"

No, I am most definitely not ready.

CHAPTER FORTY-FIVE

As the four of us walk to the room for the group therapy nobody says a word. I suppose we will be doing enough talking, and I will be the one doing most of it. It was time for me to come clean. Kelly brings us to a room a bit bigger than her usual office. The walls are white and two beige couches are lined across from one another, with a chair in the middle. Kelly sits in the chair. My mom sits on one couch, and I sit across from her. Alyssa sits down next to me, though she looks almost as nervous as I feel.

I sit frozen. Thankfully, Kelly begins the session with an introduction. She reminds everyone that this is a safe place. Then my mom does it. I think she is going to start yelling at me about my behavior. Or start questioning me because a guy was mentioned. However, my mom gives me the strength to go on with her next sentence. "Katrina, I just want you to know I love you, no matter what. We will get through this and there is nothing that you could have done that will change that."

That is when the tears come. They come in buckets, and it takes several minutes before I can speak. I did not think I would at the first, and I am grateful that Nia did not tell my mom and Alyssa everything she knew. But I must. The time has come. My voice is low as I start, but there is no turning back now. "I know burning down that shed was wrong, and Alyssa I really am not mad at you for telling my mother because it brought me here. While here I have learned that I am not alone. I think I am ready to share now what I have been going through. I think you both deserve to know." I take a deep breath before I continue. "After graduation I was in the shed with that guy... Grant. He... umm... he..." I close my eyes and tears fall silently.

"Go on Katrina," Kelly says. "We are here for you."

I take another deep breath and continue. "Grant sexually assaulted me in that shed right after graduation." I had finally spoken the words out loud. Now I waited for what comes next.

In my silence all I can hear is the gasp that falls from both Alyssa and my mother's lips. My mom now knows. What will she think of me? Tears swell in my mother's eyes, making me bow my head in shame. I cannot look at her. After a moment, I dare to lift my head, but it is not a look of shame, or resentment, or even pity that I am met with. Suddenly, my mother comes and sits on the other side of me on the couch and her arms are embracing me. Then Alyssa's arms wrap around both of us.

"This is why you burned that shed down?" my mother asks, putting the pieces of the puzzle together about why there had been such a change in the daughter she had known to the one sitting next to her now.

There is no more avoiding. I have to come clean. "Yes," I whisper, lowering my head once again.

"How scared you must have been. I am so sorry I did not see the pain you were in." My mother's words shock me.

"You are not disappointed in me?"

"What? No, baby, I could never be disappointed in you. This is not your fault. I am only sorry I did not see the pain you were in."

Alyssa looks at me and nods her head as if to agree with my mom. "Katrina, I am so sorry. As your best friend I should have known. I mean I knew something had to have happened for you to do something so drastic as to burn down a shed, but I could never have imagined what it was. Your mom is definitely right though, it is not your fault."

"If that bastard were not dead, I would kill him myself," my mother states. She is now crying almost as hard as I am. "What exactly happened?"

"I am not ready to get into the details. It has only been a couple weeks that I have faced this. I wanted you to know though. Can that be enough for now?"

My mom nods her head. "I guess it was silly of me, but on the way here I thought you may be ready to come home with me today."

"I still have a lot to work through." I debate whether to ask my mom about my dad. Perhaps, we should tackle one heavy subject at a time. It does feel like a small weight has been lifted from my shoulders, even more so than writing that letter to Alyssa. It is a one small step.

When therapy is over, I go to dinner with my mom and Alyssa. We laugh throughout most of the meal, and I even eat most of it. While at dinner I look for Scott, but I do not see him anywhere. Maybe it is for the best I do not see him with my mom just yet. I try not to think about him too much through the dinner and concentrate on my mom and my best friend. They now know what happened and they still love me. They both walk me back to my room. I know Alyssa is dying to gossip with me, I can see it written all over her face as she is taking in my new surroundings.

"The address is on the letter I gave you," I say to Alyssa. "We can write each other."

Alyssa smiles at my words. We used to be able to sense what each other were thinking, I guess we still have our bestie senses after all. "I suppose I'll take what I can get."

I turn to my mom. "I love you mom."

"I love you." She looks me right in the eyes when she says this, telling me she really means it.

I hug them each tightly before they go. I will miss them, but I know I have more work to do here before I will be ready to go back out into the world. I will still have to face Nia as well, although I do not blame her for her cousin's actions. Still, we would have to talk about it. But she would also have to wait. First, I had a good idea where Scott was, and I needed to see him.

As I rounded the side of the building the sweet scent of fresh laundry floated in the air. I made my way to the door cautiously looking out for any adult eyes. Slowly I opened the door. However, when I did my face fell along with my heart. I had found Scott alright. He sat on the couch where we had been just hours before. But he was not alone. Sitting on top of him and wearing only a black lace bra on top was Jazzie.

"Hey Katrina, aren't you going to welcome me back? Scott already did."

THE END

www.ingramcontent.com/pod-product-compliance
Ingram Content Group UK Ltd.
Pitfield, Milton Keynes, MK11 3LW, UK
UKHW020423250726
13967UKWH00007B/2784

9 781638 375630